BLACK BEAUTY

BLACK BEAUTY

According to
SPIKE MILLIGAN

This edition first published in Great Britain in 1997 by
Virgin Books
an imprint of Virgin Publishing Ltd
332 Ladbroke Grove
London W10 5AH

First published in 1996 by Virgin Publishing Ltd

A catalogue record for this book is available from the British
Library.

ISBN 0 7535 01023

Typeset by TW Typesetting, Plymouth, Devon.

Printed and bound in Great Britain by
Mackays of Chatham, Lordswood, Chatham, Kent.

PART ONE

EARLY HOME

There once was a horse called Black Beauty
He was well bred and always did his duty
He came from very good stock
He had a lovely body with a huge cock
His mother was lovely with a wonderful tail
Which dragged behind her like the Holy Grail
His father died, a handsome dude
And he ended up as dog food
Black Beauty would lead a long life
A mixture of Peace, Tranquillity and Strife.

1

MY EARLY HOME

I will always remember my early stable
We think of it when we are able
My mother was a horse
And, so was I, of course
I always stayed close to my mother
Because of horses, there were no other
I drank my mother's milk I recall
Otherwise I would have got bugger all
Oh yes, I remember when I was young
Grassy meadows, flowers and dung.

The first place that I can well remember was a large pleasant meadow with a pond of clear water full of frog spawn in which I nearly drowned. It would have been the first case of a horse drowned in frogs' spawn. Over the hedge on one side we looked on to a ploughed field where a woman was pulling a plough with a man steering it, occasionally striking the woman with a whip. It was a typical rural scene mixed with wife-beating. On the other side, we looked over a gate at my master's house. If you stood the other side, you could see us looking at our master's house. At the bottom, a steep bank overhung a running brook. Girls with babies born out of wedlock used to throw the babies in there to drown them.

Whilst I was young I lived on my mother's milk because I could not eat grass. In the daytime I ran by her side, and at night I lay down close by her side. When it was hot, we used to stand by the pond in the shade, watching the children fall in and drown. When it was cold, we had a nice warm shed.

As soon as I was old enough to eat grass, my mother used to stuff it down my throat until it kept coming out the back. I went six times that day. She was a police horse and used to go to riots and her master would bash people over their heads. I was so proud, I couldn't wait for the day when I had a rider who would bash people over the head.

I used to run with the young colts. We would frequently bite and kick.

One day there was a great deal of kicking, one or two horses were kicked unconscious. My mother whinnied to me and, as I had just been kicked unconscious as well, she ran toward me.

'Pay attention to what I am going to say'; so I paid attention. 'The colts who live here are cart-horses, and of course they have no manners. You have been well bred and well born; your father had a great name in these parts. I hope you will grow up gentle and good, lift your feet up when you trot, and never bite or kick.'

I have never forgotten my mother's advice; I knew she was a wise old horse, and our master thought a great deal of her. He thought of her when he was in the garden, he thought of her when he was in bed, and he thought of her when he was in the kitchen. He never thought of her when he was in the loo. Strange that. Her name was Duchess.

Our master was a good man, sometimes he was a good woman. Strange that. He went to church every Sunday and lit candles. Not much happened, except the church burnt down. When she saw him at the gate, she would neigh with joy, and trot up to him. He would pat and stroke her and say, 'How is your little Darkie?' I was a dull black. He would give me a piece of dry bread, the mean bugger, and sometimes he brought a carrot for my mother. Why did she do this grovelling for a bloody carrot? My mother always took him to the town on market day in a little gig.

There was a ploughboy called Dick who sometimes came into our field to pluck blackberries. When he had eaten all he wanted, he would have 'fun' with the colts, throwing stones, bricks and sticks to make them gallop. We did not much mind him, for we could gallop off; but sometimes a stone would hit and hurt us.

One day, he had just thrown a brick at my head; the master was in the next field watching, and catching Dick by the arm and his private parts, he gave him such a box on the ear and a kick up the arse. We never saw Dick any more but we heard that he joined the French Foreign Legion and was killed by an Arab who threw a brick at him. Old Daniel, who looked after the horses, was just as gentle as our master, so we were well-off.

2

THE HUNT

One day a hunt galloped thru
That is a thing they used to do
As the hunt galloped by
'Get the bastard,' was their cry
Who the bastard was they did not say
And we never found out to this very day
In fact they were chasing a hare
The trouble was, it wasn't there
Frustrated, they chased a rat
But they didn't even catch that.

Before I was two years old, something happened which I have never forgot. It was early in the spring; there must have been a little frost in the night and a light mist still hung over the plantation and meadows and hung over the house. We were feeding in the part of the field where the mist hung overhead. In the distance we heard what sounded like a cry of dogs. The oldest colt raised his head. He said, 'There are the hounds!' With the mist hanging over them we could only see their legs. We cantered off to the upper part of the field, where we could look over the hedge and see the other side. My mother and a very old riding horse in a wheel chair were standing near.

'They have found a hare,' said my mother, 'and if they come this way, we shall see the hunt.'

And soon we could only see the legs of the dogs in the mist. They were tearing down the field of young wheat next to ours. They did not bark nor howl nor whine, but kept on a 'yo! yo, o, o! yo! yo, o, o!' at the tops of their voices. Dogs who say 'yo! yo, o, o! yo! yo, o, o!' are very hard to find. Then came a number of men in green coats on horseback, all galloping as fast as they could. Some were doing 100 miles per hour and soon they were away into the fields lower down; then they seemed to lose the scent and the dogs left off yo-yoing and ran about in every direction, mostly away.

'They have lost the scent,' said the old horse, 'perhaps the hare will get off.'

'What hare?' I said.

'How do I know what bloody hare? Likely enough it may be one of our own hares; any hare will do for the dogs and men.'

And before long the dogs began their 'yo! yo, o, o!' again, and back they came, all together at full speed, making straight for the wrong way, to the part where the high bank and hedge overhung the brook.

'Now we shall see the hare,' said my mother, and just then, a hare, wild with fright, rushed by. Six or eight men leaped their horses clean over the hedge, close to the dogs. The hare tried to get through the hedge; it was too thick, and she turned sharp round to make for the road, but it was too late; the dogs were upon her with their wild cries; we heard one shriek and that was the

7

end of her. 'Heel!' said the master of hounds, and blew his horn. The hounds did not heel, seemed not to hear, and went on tearing the hare to pieces. 'Heel!' he shouted again, but they did not hear. He whipped-off the dogs, who turned on him and tore him to pieces. These were called 'sportsmen' and they were all upper class; the Prince of Wales was one of them.

Then there was a sad sight – two fine horses were down. One was struggling in the stream, and the other was groaning on the grass. One of the riders was getting out of the water covered with frog spawn and mud, the other lay quite still.

'His neck is broken,' said my mother.

'And serve him right too,' said one of the colts.

I thought the same, but my mother did not join with us.

'Well! No,' she said, 'you must not say that. Although, I never could make out why men are so fond of this sport; they often hurt themselves, they get covered in mud, they fall off and break their necks, often spoil good horses and tear up the fields, and all for a hare or a fox or a stag or an elephant, when they could get one more easily, pre-prepared and oven ready, from the butcher's.'

Whilst my mother was saying this, we stood and looked on. Many of the riders had gone to the young man, but my master, who had been watching, was the first to raise him. His head fell back and his arms hung down, his legs shot up and everyone looked very serious, especially the one with his head hanging down. There was no noise now; even the dogs were quiet, and seemed to know that something was wrong. They carried him to our master's house. It was young George Gordon, the

Squire's only son, a fine, tall young man, a cruel bastard, and the pride of his family, with his head hanging down.

They were now riding off in all directions, in fact two riders rode off in the opposite directions, to the doctor's, to the farrier's, to the butcher's, to the baker's, and no doubt to Squire Gordon's to let him know his son had snuffed it. When Mr Bond, the farrier, came to look at the black horse that lay groaning on the grass, he felt him all over, and shook his head; one of his legs was broken. Then someone ran to our master's house and came back with a gun. Presently, there was a loud bang and a dreadful shriek; Mr Bond had shot himself. And then a humanitarian put the horse down, and then all was still; the black horse moved no more.

My mother seemed much troubled. She said she had known that horse for many years. His name was Big Dick Rasputin. He was a good, bold horse, and there was no vice in him; he occasionally screwed a brood mare, that was all. She never would go to that part of the field afterwards.

Not many days after, we heard the church bell tolling for a long time. Looking over the gate, we saw a long, strange black coach that was covered with black cloth and was drawn by black horses; this was for the stiff. It was carrying young Gordon to the churchyard, to bury him. That's what happens when you die, you never ride again. What they did with Big Dick Rasputin I never knew; he was sold as dog food.

> Oh terrible ending as dog food in a tin
> It doesn't encourage a racehorse to win
> Fancy the Derby winner
> Ending up as a dog's dinner.

3

MY BREAKING IN

Oh! terrible breaking in!
It should be considered a sin
I had to gallop, walk and trot
I thought that was the lot
I was taught to go fast or slow
To stop, start and then go
A man would sit on your back
I'd take him there and bring him back
The man was Squire Gordon by name
I kicked him in the balls whenever he came
They each swole up like a marrow
He had to wheel them round on a barrow.

I was now beginning to grow handsome; some people grew up, but I grew handsome. My coat was coal black; at night people used to walk into me. Mind you, I still looked like a horse. When I was four years old, Squire Gordon came to look at me. He examined my eyes, mouth and legs. He felt them all the way down, because that's where they were. Then I had to walk and trot and gallop before him. He seemed to like me and said, 'I seem to like you. When he is broken in he will do well.'

My master said he would break me in himself, to save the expense of hiring a groom, the mean bastard! The next day he began.

Everyone may not know what breaking in is. It means you have a bloody awful time. You have to wear a saddle and carry on your back a man, woman, child, or a hundredweight sack of potatoes; or, in times of war, you have to carry a cannon. You have to learn to wear a collar. You have to be able to have a cart or a chaise fixed behind you, so that you can hardly walk without dragging it after you. It's hell I tell you. Many horses have gotten a hernia trying to pull them. You must go fast or slow, start or stop, as the driver wishes; you have no bloody choice at all. You must not speak to other horses nor bite nor kick nor crap nor have any will of your own. You might as well be bloody dead. You must do your master's will even though you may be very tired or hungry, but you can report him to the RSPCA. When the harness is once on, you may neither jump for joy nor lie down for weariness. It's a complete loss of freedom.

I had, of course, long been used to a halter and a headstall – that's a stall I sleep in with my head – and was then led about in the field and lanes, even if I didn't want to go. For those who have never had a bit in their mouths (most men have had a bit on the side), it is held fast by straps over your head, under your throat, round your nose, and under your chin, everywhere except behind your arse; so that no way in the world can you get rid of the nasty hard thing; it is very bad! Yes, very bad! But with the nice oats, and what with my master's pats, kind words, and gentle ways, I got used to wearing my bit and bridle, but it was still bloody terrible.

11

Next came the saddle, but that was not half so bad; they put it on my back, very gently, and my master got on. I immediately bolted and threw him. It certainly felt queer, but I felt rather proud to have thrown my master. However, he continued to ride me a little every day, and I would throw him every day. I soon became accustomed to it, and so did he.

Next was putting on iron shoes. The blacksmith took my feet in his hands, one after the other, and cut away some of the hoof. I stood still on three legs, sometimes two, or even one, till he had done them all. Then he clapped on a piece of iron the shape of my foot and drove some nails through the shoe into my hoof, so that the shoe was firmly on. My feet felt very stiff and heavy, but in time I got used to it.

Next was to break me to harness. First, a stiff heavy collar just on my neck. (The things they were putting on me made me weigh twelve stone more than I really was.) It was a bridle with great side-pieces against my eyes called blinkers. I could not see on either side, but only straight ahead; I kept crashing into things each side of me, one was an old lady. Next there was a small saddle strap that went under my tail; that was the crapper. I hated it; it stopped me having a crap. I never felt more like kicking, so I kicked him in the goolies and they swelled up like water melons. He had to put the harness on me while balancing his balls with one hand, and he could only move very slowly. In time I got used to everything – and he got used to swollen balls – and I could do my work as well as my mother. I used to wash up after dinner. Yes, I was a very good horse.

I must not forget to mention one part of my training. My master sent me for a fortnight to a neighbouring farm with a meadow which was skirted by railway lines. Here were some sheep and cows, and I was turned in amongst them. I couldn't help treading in it.

I shall never forget the first train. I was feeding quietly near the pales, which separated the meadow from the railway, when I heard a strange sound at a distance, and before I knew whence it came – with a rush and a clatter, and a puffing out of smoke, a long black train of something* flew by, and was gone almost before I could draw my breath. I turned, and galloped like fuck to the further side of the meadow as fast as I could go, and stood there snorting with astonishment and fear. In the course of the day many other trains went by, some more slowly; these drew up at the station close by, and sometimes made an awful shriek and groan before they stopped. They had run over a passenger.

For a few days I could not feed in peace, as passenger after passenger was run over. I began to disregard it, and very soon I got used to the sound of the train stopping and the passengers being thrown off. Now, no railway stations frighten me – not Cannon Street, Paddington or Euston.

'But,' said my mother, 'there are many kinds of men; there are good, thoughtful men like our master, who, thanks to you, has swollen balls.' She said there are many foolish men who are ignorant, who couldn't spell influenza even though they had got it. Some men were awful

*Carriages.

13

and they spoiled horses; in fact, strewn all round where we lived there were spoiled horses lying in the fields. Some men used to deliver coal and some would fall down the coal hole and were never seen again. 'Now don't forget son,' said my mother, 'do your best wherever it is, and keep up your good name.' I did, but when I felt like it I kicked them in the balls. The only respect I ever got was from men I had kicked in the balls.

4

BIRTWICK PARK

I was to work for a new master
To me, it was a disaster
In new stables I had to pass
A horse with an enormous fat arse
Ginger was his name
Alas, that's what he eventually became.

It was early in May, when there came a man from Squire Gordon's who took me away to the Hall. My master said to me, 'Good-bye, Darkie, be a good horse and always do your best; and stop kicking people in the balls.' I could not say good-bye, so I put my nose in his hand and bit off a finger. I left my first home, and as I lived some years with Squire Gordon, I may as well tell something about the place.

It was mortgaged up to the hilt. Squire Gordon's Park skirted the village of Birtwick. It was entered by a large, rusty iron gate, at which stood the first lodge, and then you trotted along on a smooth road between clumps of large old trees; then another lodge and another gate, which brought you to the house and gardens. Beyond this lay the home paddock, the old orchard, and the stables. There was accommodation for many horses and carriages and there were good stalls, large and square, each with a low rack for hay or porridge or pâté de foie gras; they were called loose boxes because, in fact, they were falling to pieces.

Into one such fine box the groom put me. He patted me, then went away. Wow, read all about it, groom pats horse and goes away! When I had eaten my corn I looked round – it must have been that bloody corn I'd eaten. Next to me was a horse with a thick mane and tail, and a pretty head.

I put my head up to the iron rails and said, 'I say, horse, pray tell me, what is your name?'

He turned round and said, 'My name is Merrylegs: I am very handsome, carry the young ladies on my back, and sometimes I take our mistress out in the low chair. They think a great deal of me, and so does James.' The bigheaded little creep! 'Are you going to live in the next box?' he asked.

I said, 'Yes.' There are fields and meadows all round but these bastards make me live in a box.

A horse's head looked over from the stall beyond.

'So it's you who has turned me out of my box; it's an outrage for a colt like you to come and turn a horse out of his own home.'

'The thing is this,' said Merrylegs, 'Ginger has the habit of biting and snapping and kicking people in the balls: that is why they call him Ginger. One day he bit James in the arm and made it bleed.' Good. 'Miss Flora and Miss Jessie, who are very fond of me, were afraid to come into the stable for fear of being kicked and bitten.

They used to bring me nice things to eat – steak and chips and spaghetti Neapolitan.'

I told him I never bit anything but grass, hay, corn and people.

'Well,' said Merrylegs, 'I don't think he does find pleasure in it.'

'Nonsense,' I said, 'there is no greater pleasure than biting and kicking people.'

'John is the best groom that ever was; he tries to please Ginger. He plays him Schumann's Violin Concerto. He has been here fourteen years and he is still as simple as when he started. He says his brain hurts if he thinks. And you never saw such a kind boy as James is; so it's all Ginger's own fault that he did not stay in that box.'

5

A FAIR START

One morning, after a grooming by John
The Squire asked him to take me on
He put on a saddle and rode very slow
So I threw him off and I jolly well did go
I galloped everywhere
But didn't seem to get anywhere
Finally knackered, I was just able
To crawl back to the stable
The stableboy James was always around
Sometimes, for fun, I would trample him into the
*   ground*
But after three weeks in hospital 'tis true
He came back, good as new.

The name of the coachman was John Manly; the name of his coach was Percy; he had a wife and one little child, and they lived in the coachman's cottage.

The next morning, he took me into the yard and gave me a good grooming, and just as I was going into my box with my coat soft and bright, the Squire came in to look at me, and seemed pleased.

'John,' he said, 'I meant to have tried the new horse

18

this morning, but I have other business. You may as well take him a round after breakfast; go by the common and the Highwood, and back by the water mill and the river, through Swansea and Kent; that will show his paces.'

'I will, sir,' said John.

After breakfast he came and fitted me with a bridle. Then he brought the saddle, which was not broad enough for my back; he saw it in a minute, and in another minute went for a bigger one, which fitted nicely. He rode me slowly at first, then a trot, then a canter, and when we were on the common, he gave me a light touch with his whip, and we had a splendid gallop at 100 miles per hour.

'Ho, ho! my boy,' he said, as he pulled me up with that powerful wrist, 'you would like to follow the hounds, I think.' The fool! I never want to follow hounds.

As we came back through the Park we met the Squire and Mrs Gordon, walking; they stopped, and John jumped off and fractured his ankle.

'Well, John, how does he go?'

'He is as fleet as a deer, and has a fine spirit too; the lightest touch of the rein will guide him but don't stand behind him or he'll kick your balls. Down at the end of the common they were shooting rabbits near the High-wood – people rarely see horses shooting rabbits. A gun went off close by so he pulled up a little and looked; it was another horse shooting rabbits. I just held the rein steady and did not hurry him, and it's my opinion he has not been frightened or ill-used while he was young.'

'That's well,' said the Squire, 'I will try him myself to-morrow.'

The next day I was brought up for my master. I

remembered my mother's counsel, and my good old master's, and I tried to do exactly what he wanted me to do. I found he was a very good rider; once or twice I threw him; landing on his head, he became an imbecile. And thoughtful for his horse too; we didn't use the crapper, so I could crap. When we came home, the lady was at the hall door as he rode up.

'Well, my dear,' she said, 'how do you like him?'

'Der he trew me on my hed,' he replied; 'pleasanter creature I never wished to mount. What shall we call him?'

'Would you like Nigger?' said she. 'He is as black as a nigger.'

'I think it is a very good name. If anyone says it, we could take them to a race relations board.'

When John went into the stable, he told James that master and mistress had chosen a good sensible English name for me: Nigger, because I was black. They both laughed, and James said, 'If it was not for bringing back the past, I should have named him Big Dick Rasputin, for I never saw two horses more alike.'

'That's no wonder,' said John, 'didn't you know that farmer Grey's old Duchess was the mother of them both?'

I had never heard that before. So poor Big Dick Rasputin, who was killed at that hunt, was my brother!

John seemed very proud of me: he used to make my mane and tail almost as smooth as a baby's bum, and he would talk to me a great deal, 'Keep still you bastard.' I grew very fond of him, he was so gentle and kind, 'Keep still you bastard'; he wanted me to keep still.

James Howard, the stable boy, was just as gentle and

pleasant in his way – 'Keep still you bastard' – so I thought myself well-off, but sometimes I would trample him into the ground. There was another man who helped in the yard sweeping up the horse dung. I didn't like him, so I did as much of it as I could.

A few days after this, I had to go out with Ginger in the carriage. I wondered how we should get on together; but except for laying his ears back and biting the driver, he behaved very well. He did his work honestly, and did his full share, usually in the middle of the road – a street cleaner used to clear it and sell it to rose growers – and I never wish to have a better partner in double harness. When we came to a hill, instead of slackening his pace, he would throw his weight right into the collar, the silly little fool, and pull away. So I let him – I just sat next to the driver. John had oftener to hold him in than to urge him forward; he never had to use the whip with either of us.

As for Merrylegs, he and I soon became great friends: we went out drinking together at the City Hall trough; he used to let me ride him. He was a favourite with everyone, except King Edward, and especially with Miss Jessie and Miss Flora, who used to ride him about in the orchard. He used to run under low branches so they would get knocked off; they had fine games with him and their little dog Frisky. He used to trample it into the mud and fracture its skull.

Our master had two other horses that stood in another stable, one on top of the other. One was Justice, a roan cob, used for riding, or for the luggage cart; the other was a very old brown hunter, named Sir Oliver, who was past it now, but was a great favourite with the master, who helped him stagger through the Park. He sometimes did a little light carting on the estate, but regularly collapsed, for he was very weak. He could be trusted with a child as long as it wasn't older than three, otherwise his legs collapsed under him; as it was, he had a pacemaker. The cob was a strong, well-made, good-tempered horse, and we sometimes had a little chat in the paddock.

'How are you?' I asked.

'I'm very well,' he answered, 'piss off, Nigger.'

6

LIBERTY

John took me out to exercise
He gripped me fast with his thighs
But I gave a huge cough
That threw him off
It gave him a shock
As he split his head open on a rock
But after three weeks in hospital 'tis true
He came back, as good as new.

I was quite happy in my new place, and all who had to do with me were good and bloody boring, forever patting me and giving me apples, and I had a light airy stable and the best of food. What more could I want? Why, liberty! For three years and a half of my life I had had all the liberty I could wish for; but now, week after week, month after month and, no doubt, year after year, I must stand up in a stable night and day except when I am wanted; sometimes I lay down which is like standing, only lower down; and then I must be just as steady and quiet as any old horse who has worked twenty years and been shot for dog food. Straps here and straps there and a thing under my arse so I couldn't shit, a bit in my mouth, and blinkers over my eyes.

Now, I am not complaining for I know it must be so.
I only mean to say that for a young horse full of strength
and spirits who has been used to some large field or
plain, where he can fling up his head, and toss up his
tail, crap and gallop away at full speed leaving the field
full of horse dung, then round and back again with a
snort to his companions – we all like to snort a joint – I
say it is hard, never to have a bit more liberty to do as
you like. Sometimes, when I had had less exercise than
usual, I felt so full of life and spring, that when John took
me out to exercise, I really could not keep quiet; I did
fifty press-ups and fifty sit-ups; do what I would, it
seemed as if I must jump, or dance – I would do the fox-
trot – or prance; and many a good shake I know I must
have given him; every now and then he would fall off,
specially at the first; but he was always good and patient.

'Steady, steady, for Christ's sake steady, my boy,' he
would say. 'Wait a bit and we'll have a good swing, and
soon get the tickle out of your feet.' What was the bloody
fool talking about? I didn't have any tickle in my feet, I
haven't got feet! Then, as soon as we were out of the village, he would give me a few miles at a spanking trot, and
then bring me back as fresh as before, only clear of the
fidgets, as he called them. Spirited horses, when not
enough exercised, are often called skittish when it is only
play, and some grooms will punish them, but our John
did not. I would come to a halt and catapult him over
my head; he knew it was only high spirits. Still, he had
his own ways of making me understand by the tone of
his voice – 'Keep still you bastard' – or by the touch of
the rein. If he was very serious and quite determined, I

always knew it by his voice, 'keep bloody still', and that had more power with me than anything else, even King George V, for I was very fond of him.

I ought to say that, sometimes, we had our liberty for a few hours; this used to be on fine Sundays in the summertime. The carriage never went out on Sundays, because the church was now a Buddhist temple.

It was a great treat for us to be turned out into the Home Paddock or the old orchard. The grass was so cool and soft to our feet, the air was so sweet, and the freedom to do as we liked was so pleasant; to gallop, to lie down, to climb a tree, and to roll over on our backs, squashing the apples. The groom had to work hard to scrape and hose them off. This was a very good time for talking. One day I said to Ginger, 'How are you getting on you old poof?' and Ginger replied, 'Not very good – I am still a bloody horse.'

7

GINGER

One day, Ginger was standing in the stable
Something which I did, when I was able
'No one,' said Ginger, 'horse, man or frog was kind to
*   me'*
I said, 'Patience, why don't you wait and see?'
I would have to bloody wait for eternity
Now Ginger wasn't very clever
He had a noisy hacking cough
Why didn't he just fuck off.

One day, when Ginger and I were standing alone in the shade, still being horses, we had a great deal of talk: he wanted to know all about my bringing up and breaking in, and I told him I'd never done a break-in.

'You see,' said Ginger, 'I was taken from my mother as soon as I was weaned and put in with a lot of other young colts: none of them cared for me and I cared for none of them, fuck 'em. There was no kind master to bring me nice things to eat like sausage and mash. The man in care of me never gave me a kind word. He didn't even say, 'fish, cupboard or teeth,' or any other words that would have been acceptable, like elephant, pudding, etc.

'A footpath ran through our field, and often boys would fling stones at us. I was never hit, but one young colt was badly cut. We settled in our minds that these boys were our enemies. We waited till they were not looking, and we rushed and then kicked them all to the death.

'We had great fun in the free meadows, galloping up and down and kicking boys to death. But when it came to breaking in, that was a bad time: several men came to catch me, and when at last they were all on my back, one caught me by the forelock and another caught me by the nose, and held it so tight that I could hardly draw my breath; yet another took my under jaw in his hard hand and wrenched my mouth open; I bit his fingers off and spat them out; and so, by force, they got the halter on and put the bar into my mouth; then, one dragged me along by the halter while another flogged my arse, and this was the first experience I had of man's unkindness.

'There was one – the old master, Mr Ryder – who I think could have brought me round when I was unconscious, and he could have done anything with me; he could have taught me petit point, chair caning and cooking. His son was called Sampson and he boasted he never found a horse that could throw him, so I did; I threw him in the river. I threw him again and again, trampling on his head till it lost its shape.

'I think he drank a great deal – he leaked – and I am quite sure that the oftener he drank, the more he leaked; he flooded the stables. One day, he worked me hard in every way, digging ditches, chopping trees and mowing the grass. I was tired and miserable and angry. Next day, he mounted me in a temper. I threw him off and rendered him unconscious by landing him on his head. He recovered consciousness, remounted me and seemed determined to stay in the saddle as he used super glue on the seat of his trousers; but I threw him, leaving the seat of his trousers on the saddle.

'At last, as the sun went down, I saw the old master coming out with a sieve in his hand. He was a very fine old gentleman with a sieve in his hand. He had white hair, and his voice had white hair. I should have known him amongst one thousand. Unfortunately he was not standing in the middle of a thousand people, so I didn't know him right away. "Come along, lassie, come along, come along," but I didn't come along lassie. What did he think I was, a dog? And hadn't he seen the size of my tackle? No, I let him come along to me. He led me back to the stable; as we arrived, there was the bastard Sampson. I snapped at him and bit his ear off. "Stand back," said the master, "you've not learned your trade yet, Sampson." His trade was, in fact, a stone mason. Why an apprentice stone mason wanted to learn to ride a horse seemed pretty pointless to me. In my stall, the old master mixed up a brandy and coke for me, which restored me no end. To Sampson he said, "If you don't break this horse in by fair means, she will never be good for anything except a hotel porter." '

8

GINGER'S STORY CONTINUED

The next time Ginger and I were in the paddock
We had been sharing a six pound haddock
He had been sold to a cruel man
A real shit called Sadistic Stan
To Ginger he was very cruel
He treated him like a mule
So Ginger started to try and bray
Day, after day, after day
It was a very good impression and eventually
Ginger kicked him in the face
And bits of him went all over the place

Ginger was a chestnut horse and he told me that a dealer had wanted another chestnut horse to match him, but the only horse they had was white, so they painted it with three coats of chestnut emulsion.

'I had been driven with a bearing rein by the dealer, and I hated it. I liked to toss my head about; I would toss it in the air and catch it as it came down. I hated to stand waiting by the hour for our mistress at some grand party or entertainment; they wouldn't let us sit down or lean against a lamp post.'

'Did not your mistress take any thought for you?' I asked. 'I mean, didn't she send out a drink and sandwiches?'

'After this, I was sent to Tattersall's to be sold; I had a label on me saying "Horse for Sale". A dealer tried me in all kinds of ways – sitting on me, standing on me, laying on me. At last they sold me for £3.00 to a gentleman in the country. His groom was hard tempered and hard handed. If I did not move in the stall when he wanted me to, he would hit me with his stable broom or feather duster, whichever came to hand. He wanted me to be afraid of him, and so he wore a series of devil masks. I bit a lump out of his arse. I made up my mind: men were natural enemies and I must defend myself, even if that meant hiring a solicitor.'

'I think it would be a real shame if you were to bite or kick John or James or the King of England.'

'I don't mean to,' he said. 'I did bite James once pretty sharp – I took three fingers off him – but John said "try him with kindness". So, instead of punishing me, James came to me with his arm in a sling and served me a whisky and soda with some little cheesy biscuits on a silver tray. I have never snapped at him since.'

Master noticed the change in Ginger – his paint was wearing off. One day, he came to speak to us, as he often did, and gave each of us a beautiful glass of Chablis.

'Aye, aye, Jim, 'tis the Birtwick balls,' said John. 'He'll be as good as Nigger by and by; kindness is all the physic he wants. All he needs is an occasional glass of Chablis.'

'Yes, sir, he's wonderfully improved, he's not the same creature that he was; he's somebody else. It's the Birtwick balls, sir,' said John, laughing.

Until then, I never knew we had Birtwick balls.

This was a little joke of John's; he used to say that a regular course of the Birtwick horse balls would cure him and any vicious horse. Where did they get a supply of Birtwick balls? The thought of grooms going round horse boxes with a pair of garden shears removing the testicles for future use is terrible. These balls, he said, were made up of patience and gentleness, firmness and petting.*

*A cover up for the act of castration.

9

MERRYLEGS

The children with Merrylegs used to play
Whether he liked it, he did not say
But he often said back in the stable
'I'd strangle them if I was able'
When he couldn't stand any more
He trampled them all over the floor
The father said, 'You'll pay for this, you'll see'
Said Merrylegs, 'No, I did it all for free.'

Mr Blomefield, the Vicar, had a large family of boys and girls; he used to fuck like a rabbit. When the children came, there was plenty of work for Merrylegs, and nothing pleased them so much as getting on him by turns and riding him all about the orchard and the home paddock, and this they would do hour after hour.

One afternoon, he had been out with them a long time, and James brought him in.

'What have you been doing, Merrylegs?' I asked.

'Oh!' said he, tossing his little head, 'I have only been giving those young people a lesson. They did not know when I had had enough, so I just pitched them off backwards; that was the only thing they could understand.'

The house, by now, was full of crippled children.

'What,' said I, 'you threw the children off? I thought you knew better than that. Did you throw Miss Jessie or Miss Flora?'

'Yes, yes. In fact, I threw them further than anybody else. I am as careful of the young ladies as the master could be, and as for the little ones, when they seemed frightened, I kicked them off. I am their best friend but sadly they don't seem to know when I have had enough, so I have to hurl them off. Each one of the children had a riding whip; I took it in good part but, Christ, it hurt. I didn't wish to be cruel, but I'm afraid some of them I put in the hospital. Besides,' he went on, 'if I took to kicking then where should I be?' I don't know but I know where they would be – in the hospital with swollen balls.

10

A TALK IN THE ORCHARD

Ginger and I were not of the carriage breed
We were built for speed
I had racehorse blood in my veins
And five pints of it
I was happy with my mistress on my back
But, alas, I didn't know the way back
I don't know which way we went
We must have driven via Surrey, Sussex and Kent.

Ginger and I were not of the regular tall carriage horse breed, we had racing blood; I had a bottle of about twelve pints in my stable. We stood about fifteen and a half hands high, but if we stood on a chair we were even taller. We were just as good for riding as we were for driving or standing on chairs. Our master used to say he disliked either horse or man who could do but one thing, like play the trombone. He would mount a horse and play the trombone. It was a spectacular sight to see him at full gallop playing 'The Flight of the Bumble Bee'. Mind you, he preferred to play it after dark, and consequently, at full gallop, he, horse and trombone went through many a plate-glass window. Our favourite practice was for me to saddle Ginger and then mount him, then put a saddle on my back and our mistress would ride on that. She could see for miles.

My mouth was so tender and my teeth had not been spoiled or hardened with McLean's toothpaste. I always used a good mouthwash after a meal – it was three-year-old Malt Whisky. Ginger did not like the bit, and Sir Oliver would say, 'There, there, don't vex yourself.' Now Ginger never vexed himself – he got another horse to do it for him.

I wondered how Sir Oliver had such a short tail. Was it an accident?

'Accident?' he snorted. 'Some cruel boys tied me up and cut off my long beautiful tail, through the flesh, and through the bone, and took it away.'

What he had left looked like a feather duster protruding from his bum. 'How,' said Oliver, 'can I ever brush flies, mice, grasshoppers, or elephants off my sides?'

'What did they do it for?' asked Ginger.

'Thieves would wear it as a disguise; they would fashion my tail into wigs and beards and rob a bank. Just fancy, somewhere in London my tail might be doing a robbery.'

Sir Oliver was a fiery old fellow; smoke used to sometimes exude from his bottom. Of course there were some nervous horses who, having been frightened, would let go a lot of dung.

'I have never let go a lot of dung,' said Sir Oliver. 'I remember one dark night, just by farmer Sparrow's house where the pond is close to the road, a hearse bearing a coffin overturned into the water. Both horses were drowned, the corpse floated away and was never seen again. Of course, after this accident, a stout white rail was put up that might be easily seen. However, a second hearse crashed through the rails, the horses were drowned, and the stiff floated away like the first one.'

When our master's carriage was overturned he said that if the lamp on the left side had not gone out, John would have seen the enormous hole the road makers left: his carriage disappeared down it and, to this day, he has never been seen again.

11

PLAIN SPEAKING

A pony was being whipped by a man
Master said, 'I'll stop him if I can
Sawyer, you shit, that pony's made of flesh and blood'
'He's no good, sir, he be a dud'
Sawyer the shit took up the reins
And my master blew out his brains
And they buried him in the garden
Where the praties grow.

The mistress was good and kind and had a large bank overdraft. She was kind to everybody, not only men and women but also horses and donkeys, dogs and cats, cattle and birds, kangaroos, buffalo and wart hogs. If any of the children in the village were known to treat any creature cruelly, she would beat them with an iron bar and hang them upside down outside for the whole day. And if somebody didn't find favour with her, she would tell her husband, and he would blow their brains out and bury them in the garden where the praties grow. Sometimes, our master weighed very heavy. Sometimes he weighed fifteen stone, and when riding me gave me curvature of the spine.

One day, he saw Sawyer ill-treating a pony. 'Sawyer, you shit!' he cried in a stern voice. 'Is that pony not made of flesh and blood?'

'Flesh and blood and temper,' said the shit.

'And do you think, you shit,' asked master firmly, 'that treatment like this will make him fond of your will?'

'I haven't made out a will yet,' said the shit.

Mr Sawyer, the shit, did not react, so my master took out a blunderbuss, blew his brains out and buried him in the garden where there was becoming less and less room. The master was much grieved by the loss of the shit. He broke down and said, 'Oh, deary me.'

One day, when he had stopped saying 'oh, deary me,' we met Captain Langley, a friend of our master's. He was driving a splendid pair of greys in a kind of brake. What kind I could not say. The master backed me a little, so as to get a good view of them.

'They are uncommonly like my wife, a very handsome pair,' he said. 'I see you have got hold of a bearing rein.'

'Yes,' said the captain. 'I like to see my horses hold their heads up.'

'You shit,' said the master, 'I think every horse should have a free head. They should be sent by parcel post to the horse in question.'

'I'll think about it,' said the captain, but as he drove away, my master took careful aim and blew the captain's brains out, and we had another grave to leap over.

12

A STORMY DAY

Oh, terrible night of storm and wind
As though the storm fiend grinned
Master had to go away
So I was in the dogcart that day
When we reached the tollgate it wasn't surprising
The tollman said the river was rising
We drove thru the water to the other side
Mostly I was under water, and nearly died
On the way back we went through a wood
'I don't think,' said John, 'we should'
Then a tearing, an oak tree crashed on the road
It missed us but hit a toad
We returned by the flooded bridge over the river
The thought made me shiver
The tollman said, 'Stop, the bridge is washed away'
'Thank god,' said John, Hip, Hip, Hooray.

One day in autumn, he called it Wednesday because that's what it was, the master had a long journey on business. I was put into the dogcart, and John went with his master. We went merrily along until we came to the tollbar, and the low wooden bridge. The river banks were rather high, and the bridge, instead of rising, went across just level, so that in the middle, if the river was full, the water would be nearly up to the woodwork and planks. However, as there were good substantial rails on each side, people did not mind it. My master's business engaged him a long time. I saw her wave him good-bye from the bedroom window.

A great rush of wind blew up and removed the seat of my master's trousers. The wind was blowing a gale against me, and I had to take two paces backward for every one forward. By the light of dawn, we arrived back.

The mistress ran out, 'Are you really safe my dear?'

'Yes, absolutely safe.'

They gave me a good feed that night; they gave me a grog of Best and a bottle of Moet et Chandon with an ice bucket.

13

THE DEVIL'S TRADE MARK

One day, John and I saw hence
A boy forcing a horse to jump a fence
He was giving the horse a thrashing
John wanted me to go and give him a bashing
Just then the horse threw him off her back
And he hit the ground with a thwack
He tried to grasp the horse's reins
But my master came and blew out his brains.

One day, John and I had been out on some business of
our master's – we were buying shares in Woolworths –
and we were returning gently, flat broke, on a long
straight road. It must have been a Roman road. At some
distance, we saw a boy try to leap a pony over a gate.
The pony would not take the leap, so the boy jumped it
for him to show him the way. Then the boy tried again,
and hit the pony with a whip, but he only turned off on
one side, scratching the boy's leg. He whipped him
again, the pony turned, and scratched his other leg.
Then the boy got off and gave the pony a hard thrashing. When we reached the spot, the pony put his head
down, threw up his heels, and hurled the boy neatly into

a hedge of nettles and, with the rein dangling from his head, he set off at a full gallop.

'Oh! oh! oh!' cried the boy, as he struggled about among the nettles, 'I say, do come and help me out.'

Then my Master rode up, dismounted, picked up his blunderbuss, and blew the boy's brains out.

'Thank ye,' said John. 'I think you are in quite the right place, and maybe a little scratching will teach him not to leap the pony over a gate that is too high for him.'

The farmer was hurrying out into the road, and his wife was standing at the gate looking frightened.

'Have you seen my boy?' said Mr Bushby as we came up. 'He went out an hour ago on my black pony.'

'Oh yes, he fell off,' said the master, 'and to put him out of his misery, I blew his brains out.'

'What do you mean?' asked the farmer.

'Well, sir, I saw your son whipping and kicking the pony, so I took careful aim and blew his brains out. It seemed to calm him, and your son is now sleeping in my garden.'

The mother began to cry, 'Oh! I must go and see my boy.'

'You will have to dig six feet down,' said John, 'that's where he is.'

We went on home, John chuckling all the way. He told James about it who laughed and said, 'Serve him right. I knew that boy at school: he took great airs on himself because he was a farmer's son; he used to swagger about and bully the little boys; of course, we elder ones would not have any of that nonsense and let him know that, in the school and playground, farmers' sons and labourers' sons were all alike, so we beat the shit out of him. I found him at a large window catching flies and pulling off their wings, so I am glad you blew his brains out.'

John said, 'There is no religion without love, and people may talk as much as they like about their religion, but if it does not teach them to be good and kind to man and beast, it is all a sham – all a sham, James, and it won't stand when things come to be turned inside out and put down for what they are.'

I personally have never had my things turned inside out, so I didn't know what he meant.

14

JAMES HOWARD

One morning, across came the master
At two miles per hour he couldn't go any faster
In his hand he held a letter
I suppose he couldn't find anything better
It was from Sir Clifford at Clifford Hall
Which, to me, meant fuck all
Sir Cliff wanted to replace his Coachman Fred
Primarily because he was dead
No one volunteered for the job
Except a bisexual called Rob.

One morning in December, John let me into my box after my daily exercise – twenty press-ups and twenty sit-ups. He was just strapping my cloth on, and James was coming in from the corn chamber with some oats, when the master came into the stable. He looked rather serious, and held an open letter in his hand. John fastened the door of my box, touched his cap, and waited for orders.

'Good morning, John,' said the master, 'I want to know if you have any complaint of James?'

'Complaint, sir? No, sir.'

'Is he industrious in his work, and respectful to you?'

'Yes, sir, always.'

'You never see him do a pee when your back is turned?'

'That, sir, I cannot swear.'

'When he goes out with the horses to exercise them, does he stop about talking to his acquaintances, or go into houses where he has no business, leaving the horses outside?'

'No, sir, he always takes the horses in with him. I will say this, sir, that a steadier, pleasanter, honester, smarter young fellow I never had. I can trust his word, and I can trust his work. Perhaps he does do a pee when I'm not looking, I know those people in laced hats and liveries, but whoever wants a character of James Howard, let them come to John Manly.'

He really was an arse licker. The old bastard had tried to find out if the young lad had ever committed something unusual, like wanking.

'James, my lad, set down the oats and come here.' So he set down the oats and came there. 'John's opinion of your character agrees so exactly with my own. John is a cautious man, when you pee against a wall he never looks. I have a letter from my brother-in-law, Sir Clifford Williams, of Clifford Hall. His old coachman, who has lived with him for twenty years, is getting feeble; his legs have dropped off and he wants a man to work with him to get into his ways, like robbing banks and interfering with little girls.'

So he would take on James.

It was settled that James should go to Clifford Hall. I

never knew the carriage to go out so often before; after yes, but never before. When the mistress did not go out, she stayed in. The master drove himself in the two-wheeled chaise. But now, whether it was the master or the young ladies, or only an errand for the master's pile ointment, Ginger and I were put into the carriage, and James drove us. At first, John rode with him on the box, telling him this and that, and after that, James drove alone.

Then, it was wonderful what a number of places the master would go to in the city on Saturdays, and what queer streets we were driven through. Every second person, in fact, was queer. He was sure to go to the railway station just as the train was coming in, and cabs and carriages, carts and omnibuses were all trying to get over the bridge together; that bridge wouldn't hold them all, for it was narrow, and many fell off. And there was a very sharp turn up to the station, where it would not have been at all difficult for people to run into each other; and so they did if they did not look sharp and keep their wits about them.

15

THE OLD OSTLER

My master wanted to visit friends forty-six miles
  away
That would take all bloody day
Next morning I was in harness, master took the rein
We grabbed a little rest on the way there
And we had to grab a little on the way back again
Master drove fast and slow
Then, to cap it all, it started to snow
When we got back I was frozen of course
And I thought, 'bugger being a horse.'

We were to visit some friends who lived forty-six miles
from our home. The first day we travelled thirty-two
miles; there were some long heavy hills, but James drove
so carefully and thoughtfully that we were not at all har-
assed. He never forgot to put on the drag as we went
downhill – he looked lovely in it and did not forget to
take it off at night. He kept our feet on the smoothest
part of the road, and if the uphill was very long, he set
the carriage wheels a little across the road, so as not to
run back, and gave us a breathing space. All these things
help a horse very much, particularly if there are kind

words in the bargain like 'Lovely, lovely, good boy, nicely,' etc.

We stopped at the principal hotel. Two ostlers came to take us out. The head ostler was a pleasant, active little man with a crooked leg. He used to play hockey with it. The man unbuckled the harness with a pat and a good word – 'fish.'

I never was cleaned so lightly and quickly as by that little old man. When he had done, James stepped up and felt me – it was lovely.

'Give me the handling of a horse for twenty minutes, and I will tell you what sort of groom he has had,' said the crooked little ostler. So they gave him a horse, but after twenty minutes he had to give up. 'I'm sorry, I have no idea what kind of a groom he had.'

16

THE FIRE

Oh, one terrible dark night I suddenly awoke
And the stable was full of the dreaded smoke
I started to choke and perspire
My arse had caught fire
When we got outside it was amazing
For the whole stable was blazing
I was lucky, I nearly died
Many were trapped who ended up fried
They ended as a hamburger on a plate
Oh, dearie me, what a terrible fate

Later in the evening, a traveller's horse was brought in by the second ostler, and whilst he was cleaning him, a young man with a pipe in his mouth lounged into the stable.

'I say, Towler,' said the ostler, 'just run up the ladder into the loft and put some hay down into this horse's rack, will you? Only lay down your pipe first.'

'All right,' said the other, and went up through the trap door; I heard him step across the floor overhead and put down the hay. James came in to look at us the last thing, and then shut the door behind him.

I cannot say how long I slept, nor what time in the

night it was, but I woke up very uncomfortable, though I hardly knew why. I got up. The air seemed all thick and choking. I heard Ginger coughing and choking; I could see nothing, but the stable was very full of smoke.

I heard a soft rushing sort of noise; I discovered it was coming out of me. And then I heard a low crackling and snapping. I did not know what it was, but a horse doesn't know everything. A horse does not know that Leonidas and his Spartans held the pass at Thermopylae against the Persian hordes.

At last I heard steps, and the ostler burst into the stable; it went all over the floor. He began to untie the horses and tried to lead them out, but he seemed in such a hurry, and so frightened himself, that he was in constant need of fresh air. The first horse would not go with him; he tried the second and third; they too would not stir. He came to me and tried to drag me out by force; of course, that was no use. He tried us all by turns and then left the stable shouting, 'All right, burn you bastards, burn!'

No doubt we were very foolish, but danger seemed to be all round, and there was nobody we knew to trust in, and all was strange and uncertain. The fresh air that had come in through the open door made it easier to breathe, but the rushing sound overhead grew louder, and as I looked upward, through the bars of my empty rack, I saw a red light flickering on the wall. Then I heard a cry of 'Fire!' outside; it wasn't outside – it was in here! The old ostler quietly and quickly came in; he got one horse out, and went to another, but the flames were playing round the trap door, and the roaring overhead was dreadful.

The next thing I heard was James's voice, quiet and cheery, as it always was.

'Come, Beauty, on with your bridle, my boy, we'll soon be out of this smother.'

It was on in no time; then he took the scarf off his neck, and tied it lightly over my eyes. The fool – I immediately walked into the wall. He led me out of the stable, crashing into everything. Safe in the yard, he slipped the scarf off my eyes, and shouted, 'Here, somebody! Take this horse while I go back for the other.'

A tall, broad man stepped forward and took me, and James darted back into the stable. I set up a shrill whinny as I saw him go. 'Ah, shut up,' said the tall, broad man.

On the other side of the yard, windows were thrown up, and people were shouting all sorts of things: 'Land ahoy!' 'God save the Queen.' A lot of good that did. Then came a cry:

'James Howard! James Howard! Are you there?'

Well, he wasn't. I heard the crash of something falling in the stable, and the next moment I gave a loud joyful neigh. 'Shut up!' said the tall, broad man. Then I saw James coming through the smoke leading Ginger. He was coughing violently and wasn't able to speak.

'My brave lad!' said the master, laying his hand on his shoulder. 'Are you hurt?'

James shook his head, for he could not speak.

'Aye,' said the big man who held me, 'he is a brave lad, and no mistake.'

I pulled myself free of the big man. I didn't like him; I bit his nose off. He put it in a handkerchief and took it away.

' 'Tis the fire engine! The fire engine!' shouted two or three voices. 'Stand back, make way!' My master didn't stand back and the fire engines ran over him. James helped him to his feet but he was covered with muck and dung and embers from his smouldering trousers. The fireman put the hose on him, and blew him out the door.

There was a dreadful sound; it was that of the horses falling from the top floor. We were taken in and well done by, with firemen playing their hoses on us all night.

The next morning, the master came to see how we were; we were soaked. James looked very happy after a visit to his mistress. His mistress was much alarmed in the night with James climbing into bed with her. Then the under ostler – there was one under ostler and one on top – said he had asked Dick go up the ladder to put down some hay, but told him to lay down his pipe first. Dick denied that his pipe had started the fire.

Two poor horses that couldn't get out were cooked to a nicety, and then exported to some French restaurants.

17

JOHN MANLY'S TALE

We went to visit a friend
Whose life was reaching its end
Master came to say good-bye
And advised him to try and not die
His doctor had said he would live for twenty years
So he need have no fears
So he got out of his bed
And stood on his head
But the blood burst a vessel in his brain
And he immediately died yet again.

The rest of our journey was very easy – we got a lift on a wagon. A little after sunset, we reached the house of my master's friend. We were taken into a clean, snug stable and a kind coachman made us very comfortable. He had put in armchairs and curtains.

'Your horses know who they can trust.'

'Yes, they could trust Queen Victoria and her ghillie John Brown who was giving it to her,' said James. 'The hardest thing in the world is to get horses out of the stable when there is a fire, flood, earthquake, hurricane, thunderstorm, plague, leprosy and toothache.'

We stopped two or three days at this place, and the stable girls gave us a relief massage. Before James left us for the night he said, 'I wonder who is coming in my place.'

'Little Joe Green at the Lodge,' said John.

'Little Joe Green! Why he's a child!'

'He is fourteen and a half,' said John, 'he is small, quick, and willing as well, and you don't tread on him. He is kindhearted too, his kidneys are kindhearted, and he has a kindhearted liver too. We were agreeable to try him for six weeks.'

'Just six weeks?' said James. 'He won't even grow an inch in that time.'

'I was never afraid of work yet,' said John, 'yet I am afraid of lions.'

'I'm frightened of ducks,' said James, 'but I'm not afraid of lions, not as long as they stay in Africa.'

'I'll just tell you how I look on these things. I was just as old as Joseph when my father and mother died of the fever, within ten days of each other. We laid odds on them as to who would go first. My father did, and I won £5.00. Then I was left with my crippled sister Nelly. Alone in the world, without a relation; I was a farmer's boy not earning enough to keep myself, much less the both of us. But our mistress (Nelly calls her an angel, and she has good right to do so), went and hired a room for her with old widow Mallet, and she gave her knitting and needlework. She taught her plumbing and made her re-plumb the house. The trouble was, when we turned the gas taps on, we got fountains of water, but out of the water tap we got gas, so we used to cook on that upside down. The master took me to the house where I had my food, my bed in the loft, a suit of clothes and three shillings a week so that I could help Nelly. Nelly couldn't help me, so I pushed her over a cliff. Nelly, who had climbed back up the cliff, was as happy as a bird. So you see, James, I'm not the man that should turn up his nose at a little boy. If you did, he would be able to see up it.'

'Then,' said James, 'you don't hold with that saying: "Everybody look after himself?"'

'Yes,' he said, 'fuck everyone else.'

James laughed at this, then he said, 'You have been my best friend, except for my mother; I hope you won't forget me.'

'No, lad, no!' said John, 'and if ever I can do you a good turn, I hope you won't forget me.'

'No, no, no, what's your name again?'

The next day Joe came to the stables to learn all he could before James left. He learned to sweep the stable and to bring in the straw and hay; he began to clean the harness, and helped to wash the carriage. As he was too short to do anything in the way of grooming, he walked underneath the horses and did what he could there.

'You see,' James said to John, 'I am leaving a great deal behind; my mother and Betsy, and you, and a good master and "mistress".' The mistress would certainly miss him. 'I will be able to help my mother much better with a new wooden leg.'

Merrylegs pined after him and went off his food. John took him out several mornings with a leading rein. He also exercised me – doing somersaults, the pole-vault, the long jump and the one hundred metres breast stroke.

Joe's father would often come in and do bugger all. He understood the work, and refused to do it.

18

GOING FOR THE DOCTOR

Oh, I was called out one early morn
Just as the day was about to dawn
Mistress kept having to go
Seventeen times an hour, she had filled the poe
Get the doctor in a hurry
And while you are out, get a takeaway curry
We all galloped like hell
When we got there, we rang the bell
'Do you know what the time is?' the doctor said
'We're all in bed'
There we were covered in mud and grime
And all he wanted to know was the bloody time
We told him our mistress was ill
Time after time the poe she would fill
The doctor attended her and I could hear him speaking
'I'm afraid, sir, your wife is leaking.'

I had eaten my hay and was lying down in my straw, fast asleep, when suddenly I was awakened by the stable bell ringing, and I heard feet running up the hall. John called out, 'Wake up, Nigger, you must go well now, if ever you did.'

'Now, John,' said the Squire, 'ride for your life; she's

had an attack on her water works. She's filled the poe seven times in the last hour.'

I galloped as fast as I could lay my feet to the ground.

When we came to the bridge, John pulled me up a little and patted my neck. 'Well done, Nigger! Good old fellow,' he said. He would have let me go slower, but my spirit was up, and I was off again as fast as before. My legs were a blur; I had never had blurred legs before. It was all quiet – everybody was asleep.

As we drew up at Dr White's, John rang the bell twice and then knocked at the door like thunder. The window was thrown up, and Dr White, in his nightcap, put his head out and said, 'What do you want?'

'Our mistress is very ill, come quickly.'

'Do you know what time it is?' asked the doctor. Here we had galloped eight miles, and all he wanted to know was the time. 'Wait,' he said, 'I will come.'

His horse was ill, so they decided to ride me. So the doctor rode off with me, leaving John with an eight hour walk ahead of him.

Soon we were at the master's house. He stood in the door with a blank cheque made out to the doctor. He had sent his son to the village to kill the money lender. I was now very ill; I must have caught something off the doctor while he was riding me.

One day, my master came to see me. 'My poor Beauty,' he said, 'you saved your mistress's life and saved us all from drowning.' Yes, I had done it for the mistress, but never again! Next time, she would have to die.

19

ONLY IGNORANCE

Oh, deary me, I have become very ill
The vet has brought me a pill
It is the size of a tennis ball
And I have to swallow it all
They started to bleed me, they took plenty
When it was finished, I was nearly bloody empty
My fever made me very sensitive to hearing
I could hear ants on the walls through a clearing
Then the vet gave me a tonic
It gave me the shits something chronic
It nearly was the death of me
So they sent me to convalesce on the Isle of Capri.

John held a pail for the bloodletting. 'You must get better soon or you are going to run out of it.' I felt very faint after it, and thought I should die. 'Yes,' they said, 'we thought you were going to die too.'

The fever made me acute of hearing. I could hear the Pope in the Vatican walking around. One night, John made me as comfortable as he could with a pillow and an eiderdown. He said he would wait half an hour to see how the medicine worked. It didn't; it gave me an attack of the shits. He sat down on a bench and put a lantern at their feet; it set fire to his trousers.

Tom Green and John had been talking. Green said, 'I wish you would say a bit of a kind word to Joe; the boy is brokenhearted, he can't eat his meals; he puts them in a drawer.' So John kindly held the boy down on his back, and forced the food down his throat.

'Now,' he said, 'if Beauty gets better, all is well, but otherwise I will say, "you bastard, you killed Nigger." '

'Well, John! Thank you. I knew you did not wish to be too hard, and I am glad you see it was only ignorance.'

'If people can say, "Oh! I did not know, I did not mean any harm," I suppose Martha Mulwash did not mean to kill that baby when she dosed it with Dalby, but she did kill it, and was tried for manslaughter. Horse slaughter is worse still,' said John. 'Aye Tom, two weeks ago, when those young ladies left your hothouse door open, with a frosty east wind blowing right in, you said it killed your crop of hothouse plants.'

'Aye, there isn't a banana that hasn't got frost bite. Worst of it is, I don't know where to go to get fresh ones. I was nearly mad.'

I heard no more, for the medicine did well and sent me to sleep, and in the morning I felt much better; but I often thought of John's words when I came to know more of the world.

20

JOE GREEN

Oh, terrible sight, a cart stuck in ruts
And the driver lashing the horses, giving them cuts
'Stop that,' said a lady with a bad cough
Whereupon the cruel driver said, 'Fuck off'
John, my groom, said, 'Stop, stop that'
But the driver knocked him flat
Nobody could stop the evil driver
Then somebody killed him with a screwdriver
The carter was buried at Hackney Wick
And they did it very quick.

Joe Green went on very well; he learned quickly. He ate
all the food he had been keeping in the drawer, and was
then violently sick.

It so happened, one morning John was out with Justice in the luggage cart, and the master wanted a note to
be taken immediately to a gentleman's house, about
three miles distant. He sent orders for Joe to saddle me
and take it; adding the caution that he was to ride carefully.

The note was delivered, and we were returning quietly, till we came to the brick field. Here, we saw a cart

heavily laden with bricks. The wheels had stuck fast in the stiff mud of some deep ruts, and the carter was shouting and flogging the two horses unmercifully. Joe pulled up. It was a sad sight. There were the two horses, straining and struggling with all their might to drag the cart out, but they could not move it; the sweat streamed from their legs and flanks, their sides heaved, and every muscle was strained – some had a prolapse – whilst the man, fiercely pulling at the head of the fore horse, swore and lashed most brutally.

'Hold hard,' said Joe, 'don't go on flogging the horses like that; the wheels are so stuck that they cannot move the cart.'

'Fuck off,' said the carter, taking no heed. He went on lashing.

'Stop! Pray stop,' said Joe. 'I'll help you to lighten the cart.'

'Mind your own business, you impudent little bastard,' and the next moment, we were going at a round gallop towards the house of the master brickmaker.

The house stood close by the roadside. Joe knocked at the door. The door was opened, and Mr Clay himself came out.

'Hulloa! Young man!'

'Mr Clay, there's a fellow in your brickyard flogging two horses to death. I told him to stop and he said "Fuck off." I have come to tell you; pray, sir, go.'

'Thank ye, my lad,' said the man, running in for his hat. Then, pausing for a moment, 'Will you give evidence of what you saw if I should bring the fellow up before a magistrate?'

'That I will,' said Joe, but the man was gone, and we were on our way home at a smart trot.

'Why, what's the matter with you, Joe? You look angry all over,' said John, as the boy flung himself from the saddle and fell into the water trough.

'I am angry all over.'

'And wet as well,' said John.

Our master, being one of the county magistrates, often had cases brought to him to settle, or to say what should be done. It was the men's dinner hour, but when Joe next came into the stable, he gave me a good-natured slap and said, 'We won't see such things done, will we, old fellow?' We heard afterwards that, because he had given his evidence so clearly, and because the horses were in such an exhausted state (they were in hospital on a drip, bearing the marks of such brutal usage), the carter was sentenced to be thrown from Beachy Head for three months.

21

THE PARTING

Everyone came to say good-bye
The queue reached as far as Rye
It even reached Bexhill
Where everybody's always ill
Queen Victoria was in the queue
Her driver was an old Jew
Hadn't any money
But was very, very funny
Merry was given to the Vicar, that was his lot
On the understanding, when he was no longer useful
He was to be shot.

We heard from time to time that our mistress was ill. The doctor was often at the house, and making a fortune. The master looked grave and anxious because he was paying. Then we heard that she must leave her home at once, and go to a warm country for two or three years, and preferably die out there. The news fell on the household like the tolling of a death-bell. Some fell on the cook, striking her on the swannicles and some fell on the footman, rendering him unconscious for life.

The first of the party who went were Miss Jessie and

Miss Flora. They came to bid us good-bye. They hugged poor Merrylegs like an old friend. Then we heard what had been arranged for us. Master had sold Ginger and me to his old friend, the Earl of Womble, for he thought we should have a good place there. Merrylegs was given to the Vicar – who baptised him into the Church of England faith – but it was on the condition that he should never be sold, and that when he was past work, he should be shot and buried. There was gratitude for you!

Joe was engaged to take care of him and to help in the house, so I thought that Merrylegs would do the washing up and the ironing.

The master was departing. 'Good-bye again,' he said, 'we shall not forget any of you,' and he got in to the carriage saying, 'Drive on, John.' Immediately he forgot them all.

The mistress walked from the carriage to the waiting room at the railway station. I heard her say in her own sweet voice, 'That clumsy, bloody husband.' Pretty soon the train came puffing up to the station, and guards were busy throwing passengers off. The doors were slammed, the guard whistled, and the train glided away.

When it was out of sight, John said, 'We shall never see her again – never. Nobody who goes to Calcutta ever comes back.' Slowly, he drove home. It wasn't our home now; it belonged to the Bradford & Bingley.

22

EARLSHALL

Oh, dear, Ginger and I are going to a new master
We fear it might be a disaster
Would he be kind or cruel?
Or would he be a bloody old fool?
He was twenty stone, alas and alack
When he sat on a horse you could hear its spine crack
He knew John Brown, the Queen's ghillie
Who wore a kilt to hide a huge willy
He had once seen the Queen
She didn't see him but she saw where he had been.

The next morning, after breakfast, Joe put Merrylegs into the mistress's low chaise to take him to the vicarage; how he enjoyed sitting in the chaise. He came first (I forget who came second), and said good-bye to us, and Merrylegs neighed to us from the yard, and a lot of bloody good it did. Then John put the saddle on Ginger and the leading rein on me, and rode us across to Earlshall Park, where the Earl of Womble lived.

There was a very fine house with a very fine 'For Sale' sign on it. It had a great deal of stabling, all with a 'To Let' sign on them. We entered the yard through a stone gateway, and John asked for Mr York. It was some time before he came – a year. He was a fine-looking, middle-aged man with the arse out of his trousers, and his voice said at once that he expected to be obeyed. 'Attention! Stand at ease!' he said. He was very friendly and polite to John. After giving us a slight look, he called a groom to take us to our boxes, and invited John to take some refreshment – a sausage and a glass of water.

We were taken to a light airy stable (mainly because it had no roof on it), and placed in boxes adjoining each other, where we were rubbed down and fed. In about half-an-hour, John and Mr York, who was to be our new coachman, came in to see us.

'Now, Mr Manly,' he said, 'Stand at ease! Attention! Slope arms! I can see no fault in these horses, but we all know that horses have their peculiarities as well as men, and that sometimes they need different treatment; I should like to know if there is anything particular in either of these that you would like to mention.'

'Well,' said John, 'I do not believe there is a better pair of horses in the country. They occasionally like a banana frappé with a glass of brandy. But the chestnut, I fancy, must have had bad treatment; for three years I have never seen the smallest sign of temper, but he is naturally of a more irritable constitution than the black horse. Flies tease him more, tigers terrify him; anything wrong in the harness frets him more; and if he is ill-used or unfairly treated, that means a kick in the balls and biting your nose.'

They were going out of the stable when John stopped and said, 'I had better mention that we have never used the bearing rein.'

'Fuck them,' said York, 'if they come here, they must wear the bearing rein.'

'I am sorry for it, very sorry,' said John, 'but I must go now, or I shall lose the train.' He has never been seen since.

The next day, Lord Womble came to look at us; he seemed pleased with our appearance, but we could not say the same for him with his arse out of his trousers.

'I have great confidence in these horses,' he said, 'from the character my friend, Mr Gordon, has given me of them. Of course, they are not a match in colour, but my idea is that they will do very well for the carriage whilst we are in the country. Before we go to London I must try to match Baron. The black horse, I believe, is perfect for riding.'

York then told him what John had said about us.

'Well,' said he, 'you must keep an eye to the one who knocks you on the balls, and put the bearing rein easy, otherwise your balls are for it. I dare say they will do well with a little humouring at first. Frightened of tigers, eh? He likes a bubble bath.'

In the afternoon, we were harnessed and put in the carriage, and as the stable clock struck three, we were led round to the front of the house. Two footmen were standing ready, dressed in drab livery, with scarlet breeches and white stockings. Presently, we heard the rustling sound of silk as my lady came down the flight of stone steps. She fell all the way from the top to the bottom. She stepped round to look at us. She was a tall, proud-looking woman with a face like a dog's bum with a hat on, and did not seem pleased about something, but she said nothing, and got into the carriage.

This was the first time of wearing a bearing rein, and I must say, though it certainly was a nuisance not to be able to get my head down now and then, it did not pull my head higher than I was accustomed to carrying it. I felt anxious about Ginger, but he seemed to be quiet and content.

The next day, at three o'clock, we were again at the door, and the footmen were as before; we heard the silk dress rustle, and the lady fell down the steps from top to bottom, and in an imperious voice she said, 'York, you must put those horses' heads higher.'

York bent down and said, 'I beg your pardon, my lady, but these horses have not been reined up for three years, and my lord said it would be safer to bring them to it by degrees; but if your ladyship pleases, I can take them up a little more.'

'Do so,' she said.

Day by day, hole by hole, our bearing reins were shortened, until I was permanently looking up. Ginger too seemed restless, though he said very little. But the worst was yet to come.

23

A STRIKE FOR LIBERTY

My lady said, 'Are you never going to get those horses
*   heads up, I say?'*
My head was drawn back till it was facing the other
*   way*
When they tried it on Ginger
His groom for he did to injure
He kicked the carriage to bits
It gave the terrified passenger the shits
They never put on the tight rein again
The weather forecast was for rain.

One day, my lady fell down the stairs later than usual and the silk rustled more than ever.

'Drive to the Duchess's,' she said. 'Are you never going to get those horses' heads up, York? Raise them at once, prop them up with a stick.'

York came to me first, whilst the groom stood at Ginger's head. He drew my head back until it was facing the other way, and fixed the rein so tight that it was almost intolerable. Then he went to Ginger, who was impatiently jerking his head up and down against the bit, as was his way now. He had a good idea of what was coming, and the moment York took the rein off the terret in order to shorten it, he took this opportunity, and reared up so suddenly that York had his nose roughly hit, and his hat knocked off; the groom was thrown off his legs. At once, they both flew to his head, but he was a match for them, and went on plunging, rearing, and kicking in a most desperate manner; at last, he kicked right over the carriage pole and fell down, after giving me a severe blow on my near quarter. There is no knowing what further mischief he might have done, had not York promptly sat himself down flat on his head.

'Unbuckle the black horse! Cut the trace here, somebody, if you can't unhitch it.'

One of the footmen ran for the winch, and another brought a knife from the house. The groom soon set me free from Ginger and the carriage, and led me to my box.

Ginger, the bugger, was led away by two grooms, a good deal knocked about and bruised. York went with him and gave his orders, and then came back to look at me. In a moment, he let down my head.

'Well, old chap,' York said, 'you have taken a real beating.'

He felt me all over, and soon found the place above my hock where I had been kicked. It was swollen and painful, and he ordered it to be sponged with hot water. A lot of bloody good that did.

His lordship was much put out when he learned what had happened. He blamed York for giving way to his mistress, to which he replied that in future he would much prefer his lordship to tell her, but I think nothing came of it because things went on the same as before, except the mistress split his lordship's head with an iron bar.

Ginger was never put in the carriage again. One of the lordship's younger sons said he would like to have him and make him a good hunter. As for me, I was obliged still to go in the carriage and had a fresh partner called Max; he had always been used to the tight rein. I asked him how it was he bore it.

'Well,' he said, 'I bear it because I bloody well have to, but it is shortening my life, and it will shorten yours too, if you have to stick to it.'

'Do you think,' I asked, 'that our masters know how bad it is for us?'

'I can't say,' he replied, so he did not say.

What I suffered with that rein for four long months in my lady's carriage! Before that, I never knew what it was to foam at the mouth, but now people saw it and shouted, 'rabies!' We did have a stable boy who foamed at the mouth; he had rabies and they shot him.

24

THE LADY ANNE

I became the favourite of Lady Anne
She was built like a brick shit house with a face like a
*   man*
She got me out, each freezing dawn
And I wished to Christ I'd never been born
But now of course
I was pissed off being a horse
Why wasn't I born a cheetah
Then I could eat her.

The Lady Harriet, who remained at the Hall, was a great invalid; she became an official invalid and never went out in the carriage, only on a stretcher. Lady Anne preferred riding horseback with her brother, or cousins. They were, in fact, all a collection of louts. She chose me for her brother and cousins, and named me Black Auster. I enjoyed these rides very much in the clear cold air, sometimes with Ginger, sometimes with Lizzie. This Lizzie was a bright bay mare, almost thoroughbred, and a great favourite with the gentlemen on account of her fine action and lively spirit.

There was a gentleman by the name of Blantyre staying at the Hall who always rode Lizzie and fucked Lady Anne and praised her so much that one day, Lady Anne ordered the side saddle to be put on and Lord Blantyre mounted, and slid off.

'Let me advise you not to mount her,' he said, 'she is a charming creature, but she's too nervous for a lady.'

'Oh,' said Lady Anne, 'I have been a horsewoman ever since I was a baby.'

'No more,' he said.

He placed her carefully on the saddle and gave the reins gently into her hands, then mounted me. Just as we were moving off, a footman came out with a foot and a slip of paper and a message from the Lady Harriet – 'Would they ask this question for her at Dr Ashley's and bring the answer?'

The village was about a mile off, and the doctor's house was the last one in it. We went along gaily till we came to his gate. Blantyre alighted at the gate, and was going to open it for Lady Anne, but she said, 'I will wait for you here, and you can hang Auster's rein on the gate.'

He hung my rein on one of the iron spikes, and was soon hidden amongst the trees. My young mistress was sitting easily, humming a little song:

'I've got a lovely bunch of coconuts, see them all standing in a row, big ones, small ones, someone's been in your head.'

Suddenly, a huntsman in the field discharged a gun. The horse gave a violent kick and dashed off in a head-long gallop. Blantyre came running to the gate; in an instant he sprang into the saddle, and fell off the other side.

For about a mile and a half we galloped, then we saw a woman standing at her garden gate, shading her eyes with her hand. Scarcely drawing the rein, Blantyre shouted, 'Which way?' 'To the right,' she shouted pointing with her banana, and away we went. An old road-mender was standing near a heap of stones – his shovel dropped, and his hands raised. He mistook my master for a highwayman, and master took advantage of it to remove his wallet.

He chased after my lady and I prayed her horse would fall and Lady Anne would be killed or, if not, terribly injured. To my delight, we found that she had, indeed, been thrown. The young mistress lay motionless, please God she was dead. The groom came to help Lady Anne.

'I'll never ride that fucking horse again,' she said, and fell back.

'Annie, dear Annie, do speak!' said Blantyre.

The fool, people can't speak when they're unconscious. He unbuttoned her habit, loosened her collar, and felt her tits.

Two men cutting turf came running. The foremost man seemed much troubled at the sight and asked what he could do.

'Well,' said Blantyre, 'you can feel her tits before she becomes conscious.'

'Well, sir, I bean't much of a horseman, but I'd risk my neck for the Lady Anne. She was uncommon good to my wife in the winter and lent us her tomato sauce.'

'Then mind my horse, call the doctor and alert the house.'

'All right, sir, I'll do my best, and I pray God the dear young lady will open her eyes soon.' Then seeing the other man, he called out, 'Here, Joe, feel her tits before she becomes conscious!'

He then scrambled into the saddle. I shook him as little as I could help, but once or twice on rough ground he called out, 'Steady! Woah! Steady! For Christ's sake, woah!' On the high road we were all right, and at the doctor's and the Hall he did his errand like a good man and true. 'If you hurry, doctor, you can feel her tits before she becomes conscious.'

The doctor arrived. He poured something into her mouth and it all drained out the other end.

Two days after the accident, Blantyre paid me a visit; he patted me and praised me and gave me some fish and chips.

25

REUBEN SMITH

A few words on Reuben Smith
Who was always out on the pissith
He looked after my stable
That is, whenever he was able
He was a very fine farrier
And also an Aids carrier
He said he caught it off a toilet seat in Bombay
So he caught his Aids from far away
However he won't live long
But to bury him before he died would be very wrong.

No one understood horses more than Reuben Smith. There could not have been a more faithful or valuable man. Some valued him at over £100. He could walk on his hands, waggle his ears, and juggle coconuts, of which he had a lovely bunch. With four in hand and two in the other he was the complete piss artist. When he was pissed, his favourite trick was to urinate through people's letter boxes. He was a terror to his wife; his underpants took the brunt of it.

York had hushed the matter up, at the same time rendering him unconscious with an iron bar: one night, he had to drive a party home; he was so drunk, he couldn't hold the reins and fell off the driving seat and into the gutter, where he became covered in it. This affair could not be hidden, but you could smell it on him. He was dismissed; his poor wife and little children were turned out of the cottage they lived in, so he booked them into the Savoy Hotel in London and put it on Lord Grey's bill. But Lord Grey forgave him on the understanding that he would never taste another drop as long as he lived.

Colonel Blantyre had to return to his regiment. At the station, he pressed a penny into Smith's hand. 'The mean bastard,' said Reuben Smith, and bid him good-bye.

Then he drove to the White Lion and told the ostler to have me ready at four o'clock. But it came four o'clock, and five, and then he shouted not till six, as he'd met with some old friends. Finally, he appeared at nine o'clock, pissed out of his mind and sick all down the front.

The landlord stood at the door and said, 'Have a care, Mr Smith!'

'Fuck off!' said Mr Smith.

He was forced to gallop at my utmost speed, 150 miles per hour. 'Faster, 160 miles per hour!' I stumbled and fell with violence on both my knees. Smith was flung off by my fall, and owing to the speed I was going at, he must have fallen with great force. The moon had just risen above the hedge, and by its light I could see Smith lying a few yards beyond the hedge with sick all down the front. He did not rise, he made one slight effort to do so, and then there was a heavy groan. I could have groaned too, so I did. I groaned and he groaned, and then we took it in turns to groan. Finally, we heard the sound of horse's hooves. It was a lovely summer night and I could hear the nightingale, only interrupted now and then by the sound of Smith being sick.

26

HOW IT ENDED

One night I heard horse's feet
They came from the street
Then, oh, woe is me
There happened a tragic tragedy
They found a dark figure on the ground
From which there came not a sound
One man turned him over
' 'Tis Reuben Smith,' he said
'And what's worse, he's dead'
So he died from alcohol
And Aids he caught from Deptford Mall
He will be greatly missed
One blessing was, never again would he be pissed.

It must have been nearly midnight when I heard, at a great distance, the sound of horse's hooves. They came slowly, and stopped at the dark figure that lay on the ground.

One of the men jumped out. 'It is Reuben!' he said, 'and he does not stir.'

They raised him up, then they laid him down again, and then for fun they picked him up and laid him down again.

'I have just seen your cut knees,' they said.

'Yes, nasty aren't they?' I said.

Robert attempted to lead me forward. I made a step but almost fell again, so he tried leading me backwards.

'Hallo! He's bad in his foot as well as his knees – his hoof is cut all to pieces! I tell you what!'

'Tell me what?' said Ned.

'I tell you what – either Reuben or the horse was pissed.'

Reuben was now breathing his last, and they all gathered round so as not to miss any of it. It was agreed that Robert, as the groom, should lead me, and that Reuben would be put in the dogcart. This wasn't easy; they had to double him up with his legs sticking under his chin.

Robert came and looked at my foot again, and must have felt sorry for me because they gave me tea and a sandwich. At last I reached my own box, and Reuben was put in his box, which unlike mine, was going underground.

When at last my knees were healed, they put a blistering fluid over both of them; alas, I will always have bald knees.

27

RUINED AND GOING DOWNHILL

As soon as my knees get better
I am going to write my mother a state-of-knees letter
I was put in a meadow, all alone
I longed for company, even an old ageing crone
I was able to eat great amounts of grass
All it did was go straight thru me and out my arse
One day, my friend Ginger came on the scene
He was nothing like the horse he had been
He was so very thin
Actually, you could see right in
Lord George had ridden him into the ground
So deep, he couldn't be found
He became very, very ill
Ruined and going downhill.

As soon as my knees were healed, I was turned into a small meadow; after a month I was turned back into a horse again. I felt very lonely; I felt my legs, and they felt lonely. Ginger and I had become fast friends; we did 45 miles per hour.

One day, in came dear old Ginger, and with a joyful whinny, I trotted up to him. We were both glad to meet, but I soon found that it wasn't for our pleasure he was brought to be with me. The story would be too long to tell, at least three months, but the end of it was that he had been ruined by hard riding, and was now turned off, to see what rest would do. Would he become dog food?

Soon after I left the stable there was a steeplechase. Lord George was determined to ride, and the groom told him he was a little strained, and not fit for the race. On the day of the race he came in with the first three horses, but his wind was touched; it was escaping out the back.

One day, the Earl came into the meadow, and York was with him. Fuck them! He examined me and said, 'I can't have knees like these in my stables.'

Knees

You've got to have knees
They're the things that take stock when you sneeze
You've got to have knees
They only come in fours, but never threes
You've got to have knees
In the winter, fill them up with anti-freeze
You've got to have knees
Famous for having them are bees
You've got to have knees
If you want to see mine, say please
You've got to have knees
They help you run away from falling trees
Knees – wonderful knees!

'No, my lord, of course not,' said York, the grovelling little bastard.

'They'll soon take you away,' said Ginger. 'It's a hard world.'

I tested the ground with my hoof; yes, indeed, the world was very hard.

Through the recommendation of York, the bastard, I was bought by the master of the livery stables. I found myself in a comfortable stable, and well attended to. There were some nice pictures on the wall and a three-piece suite.

28

A JOB-HORSE AND HIS DRIVERS

I've always been driven by people
Of which there are a few
They were English, Irish, Chinese and even a Jew
Some drivers have no control over their horse
I had a driver who did not know his left from his right
So he drove me in bloody circles all bloody night
Some drivers are insane, and not to blame
They can be driving, and are never seen again.

Some poor horses have been made hard and insensible
by just such drivers as these, and may, perhaps, find
some support in it; but for a horse, you can depend upon
its own legs. My motto is, 'Never use a horse without his
own legs.' Some drivers fall asleep; some used to fall
backwards in the carriage and get carried away.

Drivers are often careless and will attend to anything
else rather than their horses, like a woman with no
knickers. My driver was laughing and joking with the
lady with no knickers. He was sitting next to her and
feeling her all over, and thus we drove into a shop window. 'Now look what you've done,' said the driver, 'I've
had to stop my groping.' A farmer helped me out of the

shop window. He put me in my stable that night, but he went off and continued groping.

29

COCKNEYS

Some people like to drive us like a steam train
They make us eat lumps of coal again and again
Eating coal we were fit to bust
Eventually it shot out the back as dust
My best master was Farmer Cray
Even he turned out to be gay
He carried a pot of Vaseline
You couldn't tell where he was, but you could smell
*   where he had been.*

There is a steam engine style of driving, and these drivers keep shouting 'choo-choo-choo-choo.' People never think of getting out to walk up a steep hill, yet we have to.

Another thing, however steep the downhill may be, they scarcely ever put on drag; one or two men put on the top and skirts and stockings and go looking for sailors.

These Cockneys, instead of starting at an easy pace, generally set off at full speed from the stable yard, some at 100 miles per hour. Some go so fast, we go past where we are going, and have to start all over again. And some of them, they call that pulling up with a dash. We call it fucking awful. And when they turn a corner, they do so so sharply, we end up facing the other way.

As we were near the corner, I heard a horse and two wheels coming rapidly down the hill towards us. We had no time to pull up. The whole shock came upon Rory. The gig shaft ran right through his chest making him stagger back with a cry. It was a long time before the wound healed – five years. He was sold for coal carting; and what that is, is up and down those steep hills; they were delivering in the Himalayas.

I went in the carriage with a mare named Peggy. She was a strong, well-made animal, of a bright dun colour, beautifully dappled, and with a dark brown mane and tail. She was very pretty, remarkably sweet-tempered and willing – so I screwed her. Still, there was an anxious look about her eye. She had some trouble; it was me. The first time we went out to dinner together, I thought she had a very odd pace; she seemed to go partly in a trot, partly in a canter – three or four paces, and then to make a little jump forward. It threw the food all over us.

'How is it,' I asked, 'you are so strong and good tempered and willing?'

'I was sold to a farmer,' she said, 'and I think this one was a low sort of man. One dark night, he was galloping home as usual, when all of a sudden the wheel came against some great heavy thing in the road – it was an elephant – and turned the gig over in a minute. He was thrown out and his arm was broken, and some of his ribs.'

After she left us, another horse came in. He was

young, and had a bad name for shying and starting. I asked him why.

'Well, I hardly know,' he said; 'I was timid when I was young, and was a good deal frightened several times, and if I saw anything strange, like a rhino or water buffalo, I used to turn and look at it. You see, with our blinkers on, one can't see or understand what a thing is unless one looks round; so my head was back to front and I was crashing into buildings. I am very frightened of lions and wolves. I know Mrs Brown, and I am not frightened of her.'

One morning, I was put in a light gig and taken to a house in Pulteney Street. Two gentlemen came out, one short and one tall, as is often the case in England.

'Do you consider this horse wants a curb?' he said to the ostler.

I was eventually sold to Mr Barry.

30

A THIEF

One day a friend said to my master
'Can't he go any faster?
The reason is, standing still
He looks quite ill'
Truth was, my groom was selling my corn and giving
*   me grass*
So my master kicked his arse.

My new master was an unmarried man. His doctor advised him to take horse exercise, so for miles he galloped along like a horse, and finally exhausted, he bought me. He hired a man called Filcher to work as a groom, or a man called Groom to work as a filcher. He ordered the best hay with plenty of oats, crushed beans, rye grass and Whitstable oysters.

One afternoon, we went to see a friend of his – a gentleman farmer. This gentleman had a very quick eye for horses; it did 30 miles per hour. After he had welcomed his friend he said, 'It seems to me, Barry, that your horse does not look so well; has he been well?'

'Yes, I believe so,' said my master, who believed so.

'My groom tells me that horses are always dull in the autumn, and that I must expect it.'

'Autumn! Fiddlesticks! Bollocks!' said the farmer.

'Please don't swear in front of the horses,' said my master.

'Why this is only August; and with your light work and good food he ought not to go down like this, even if it was autumn. How do you feed him?'

My master told him. The other shook his head slowly, and began to feel me over.

'I can't say who eats your corn, my dear fellow, but your horse doesn't get it. Have you ridden very fast? I hate to be suspicious, and, thank heaven,' So my master thanked heaven. 'I have no cause to be, for I can trust my men; but there are mean scoundrels, wicked enough to eat a dumb beast's share of food; you must look into it.' And turning to his man who had come to take me: 'Give this horse a right good feed of bruised oats topped with some oysters.'

Five or six mornings after this, just as the boy had left the stable, the door was pushed open and a policeman walked in, holding the child tight by the arm; another policeman followed, and locked the door on the inside, saying, 'Show me the place where your father keeps his rabbits' food.'

The boy looked very frightened and wet his pants. But there was no escape, and he led the way to the corn bin. Here the policeman found another empty bag like that which was found full of oats and oysters in the boy's basket.

Filcher was cleaning my feet at the time, but they soon

saw him, and though he blustered a good deal, they walked him off to the lock-up, and his boy with him. I heard afterwards that the boy was not held to be guilty, but the man was sentenced to prison for two months, one oyster a day for life and a year in a lion cage.

31

A HUMBUG

One day came a new groom, Alfred Smirk
In rhyming slang he was a berk
He never changed the straw in my stall
Overpowering was the smell of my dung that I let fall
Master said, 'That smell is shit
Go get rid of it'
So Alfred got rid of the smell and the flies
Then my master shot him between the eyes.

In a few days, a new groom came. If ever there was a humbug in the shape of a groom, Alfred Smirk was the man. He was in the shape of a groom.

Alfred Smirk considered himself very handsome; he spent a great deal of time about his hair, whiskers and necktie before a little looking glass in the harness room. Everyone thought he was a very nice young man, and that Mr Barry was very fortunate to meet with him. I would say he was the laziest, most conceited bastard I ever came near. Of course it was a great thing not to be ill-used, but then a horse wants more than that. He wants music, champagne and dancing. I had a loose box, so loose it was falling to bits, and might have been very comfortable, if he had not been too indolent to clean it out. He never took all the straw away, and the smell from what lay underneath was very bad, while the strong vapours that rose up made my eyes water.

One day, the master came in and said, 'Alfred, the stable smells rather strong. I'd say it was shit. Should not you give that stall a good scrub, and throw down plenty of water?'

'Well, sir,' he said, touching his cap, 'throwing down water in a horse's box, they are very apt to take cold, sir.'

'Well,' said the master, 'I should not like him to take cold, but I don't like the smell of horse shit; do you think the drains are all right?'

'Well, sir, now you mention it, the drain does sometimes send back a smell; there may be something wrong, sir.'

'Then send for a bricklayer,' said the master.

The bricklayer came and pulled up a great many bricks and found nothing amiss; so he put down some lime and charged the master five shillings, and the smell in my box was as bad as ever. Mind you some of the smell was Alfred Smirk. Standing, as I did, on a quantity of my own crap, my feet grew unhealthy and tender, and the master used to say:

'I don't know what is the matter with this horse, he goes very fumble-footed.'

'Yes, sir,' said Alfred, 'I have noticed the same myself.' The bastard.

Now the fact was, he hardly ever exercised me, except for knee-bends and press-ups. This often disordered my stomach, and sometimes made me heavy and dull with the shits, but more often restless and feverish. I had to take horse balls and draughts, which, beside the nuisance of having them poured down my throat, used to make me feel ill and uncomfortable, and more shits.

My master stopped at the farrier's and asked him to see what was the matter with me. The man took up my feet one by one and examined them; then, standing up, he said:

'Your horse has got the thrush, and badly too.'

Not only had I got thrush, but badly, too.

'If you will send him here tomorrow, I will attend to the hoof.'

The next day I had my feet thoroughly cleansed and stuffed with tow soaked in some strong Harpic, and a very unpleasant business it was.

With this treatment, I soon regained my spirits, and threw my master. Mr Barry was so much disgusted at being twice deceived by his groom that I was therefore sold again. My master poured petrol on Alfred Smirk's balls and set fire to them.

32

A HORSE FAIR

I had a 'Horse for Sale' ticket tied on me
A man called Jim said, 'I'll give £23 for thee'
Master said, 'you will have to up your offer, Jim'
'Up yours,' replied Jim
Then he walked away
And has never been seen again to this day.

No doubt, a horse fair is an amusing place to those who have nothing to lose; if they do lose something they just have to go and look for it.

Long strings of young horses out of the country, droves of shaggy little Welsh ponies who all played rugby, and hundreds of cart horses, some of them with their long tails braided up and tied with scarlet cord. Round in the background there were a number of poor things, sadly worn down with hard work as if there was no more pleasure in life for them. They were all, in fact, being sold for dog food. There were some so thin, you could see inside them.

There was a great deal of bargaining; a man pulled open my mouth, and then looked at my eyes. With my mouth open, they could see straight away through to the coast of France. One man came to bid for me. He was very quick with his motions, and I never knew exactly where they were. He had that lovely clean smell of somebody who always used Sunlight soap, as if he had just come from a laundry. He offered £23 pounds for me; but that was refused, and he walked away. I looked after him. A very hard-looking man with acne came; I was very afraid that he would have me, but he walked off. Just then, the grey-eyed man came back again. I could not help reaching out my head towards him.

'Well, old chap,' he said, 'I think we should suit each other. I'll give twenty-four for him.'

'Say twenty-five and you shall have him.'

'Twenty-four ten,' said my friend, 'and not another sixpence, yes or no?'

'Done,' said the salesman, 'and you may depend upon it: there's a monstrous deal of quality in that horse.'

The money was paid on the spot; it was a spot of three inches in diameter. He led me to an inn called The Flat Hedgehog, gave me a good feed of oats, and stood by whilst I ate it, talking to himself, and to a tree. Half-an-hour after, we were on our way to London, through pleasant lanes and flooded roads. Half-an-hour later, we came to the great London thoroughfare on which we travelled steadily until, half-an-hour later, we reached the great city. The gas lamps were already lighted; there were streets to the right, and streets to the left, and streets crossing each other, and streets that went straight up for mile upon mile. I thought the corner to the right went into the Valley of Death, and we should never get to the end of them. At last, charged the gallant six hundred, bravely they rode and well. Passing through one street, we came to a long cab stand, but what was that terrible smell? My rider called out in a cheery voice, 'Good night, Governor.' As the Governor lived thirty miles away, he had little chance of hearing it. So rode the gallant six hundred.

'Halloo,' cried a voice, 'have you got a good one?'

'Yes,' replied my owner, 'but I'm not going to show it with all these people.' And he rode on.

Half-an-hour later, my owner pulled up at one of the houses and whistled. The door flew open, the cat flew out, followed by a young woman, followed by a little girl and boy. There was a very lively greeting as my rider dismounted. The boy stood on his mother's head, and the little girl on the boy's head; they were a family of acrobats.

'Now, then, Harry, my boy, open the gates and mother will bring us the lantern.'

The next minute, they were all standing round me in a small stable yard.

'Is he gentle, father?'

'Yes, Dolly, as gentle as your own kitten.'

At once, the little hand was patting about all over my shoulders without fear. How good it felt!

'Let me get him a bran mash and oysters while you rub him down,' said the mother.

'Do, Polly, it's just what he wants, and I know you've got a beautiful mash and oysters ready for me.'

33

A LONDON CAB HORSE

My master's name was Jeremiah Barker
He was a silly farker
His wife was a tidy woman with a huge bum
Which Jeremiah beat as a drum
Boom – Boom – Boom
It echoes round the room
My new name was Jack
Perfect for a horse who was jet black
Another horse had been in action in the Crimea
And had shrapnel
So it came to pass
He had a sore arse.

My new master's name was Jeremiah Barker, but everyone called him Jeremiah Barker. Polly, his wife, was just as good a match as a man could have. She was plump and had a moustache, a trim, tidy little woman, with smooth dark hair, dark eyes and a huge bum. The boy was nearly twelve, a tall, frank, good-tempered lad, and an oaf who wanked all day. Little Dorothy was her mother over again, at eight years old with a big bum. They were all wonderfully fond of each other; I never knew such a happy, merry family before, or since.

Jeremiah Barker had a cab of his own, and two horses, which he drove and attended to himself. His other horse was a tall, white, rather large-boned animal, called Captain; he had him when he was a Private. He was old now, but when he was young he must have been splendid; he had still a proud way of holding his head and arching his neck; in fact, he was a high-bred, fine-mannered, noble old horse, every inch of him. He told me that in his early youth he went off to the Crimean War. Bravely they rode and well, into the valley of hell. He belonged to an officer in the cavalry, and rode with the gallant six hundred. 'Their's is not to reason why, their's is but to do and die.' I will tell more of this hereafter; if there is a hereafter.

The next morning, when I was well groomed, Polly and Dolly came into the yard to see me, and make friends. Harry had been helping his father since the early morning, standing on his head.

'We'll call him Jack,' said Jeremiah, 'after the old one – shall we, Polly?'

'Do,' she said, 'for I like to keep a good name going.'

So, from Black Beauty, to Nigger, to Black Auster, and now Jack. What would it be next – Dick?

After driving through the side street, we came to a large cab stand. On one side of this wide street was an old church and old churchyard, surrounded by old iron palisades. Why? No one inside wanted to get out, and no one outside wanted to get in. We pulled up at the rank. Two or three men came round and began to look at me and pass their remarks.

'Good for a funeral,' said one – the bastard!

'Too smart-looking,' said another, shaking his head

which rattled. 'You'll find out something wrong one of these fine mornings, or my name isn't Jones.' His name wasn't Jones; it was Starbruckenborg.

The first week of my life as a cab horse was very trying; I tried to be a cab horse. Even when we were standing still on the spot.

In a short time, I and my master understood each other as well as a horse and man could do. Sometimes, he would let me wear one of his shirts. Even in the stable he did everything he could for our comfort. He put in an armchair and a bar. He took off our halters and put the bars up the windows, and thus we could turn about or stand, whichever way we pleased. I used to go clockwise. He always gave us plenty of clean water, which he allowed to stand beside us both night and day. Yes, we slept with water standing beside us – big deal!

34

AN OLD WAR HORSE

Captain was in the charge of the light brigade
Cannons to the right of them
Cannons to the left of them
Cannons underneath them
Cannons over the top of them
While horse and hero fell
What was that terrible smell
Bravely they rode well
But what was that terrible smell
They charged the Russian guns
Which gave some of them the runs
Some of the Russians went spare
Looking for clean underwear
They charged into the mouth of hell
They flashed the sabres bare
Nobody at home seemed to care
Thru shot and shell
But what was that terrible smell
It was the gallant six hundred.

Captain had been broken in and trained for an army horse, but he started as a private. He told me he thought the life of an army horse was very pleasant, but when he came to be sent abroad:

'That part of it,' he said, 'was dreadful! Of course we could not walk into the ship. We were lifted off our legs and swung to the deck of the great vessel. Then we were placed in small close stalls, and never for a long time saw the sky, or were able to stretch our legs. Somehow I managed to stretch mine an extra three inches. The ship sometimes rolled about in high winds, and we were knocked about. Many horses were sick and felt bad. I felt myself, and I felt bad.

'We soon found that the country we had come to was very different from our own. The men were so fond of their horses, they did everything they could to make them comfortable, in spite of snow. They all let us sleep in their beds with them.'

'But what about the fighting?' I asked, 'Was that not worse than anything else?'

'Well,' said he, 'I hardly know. We always liked to hear the trumpets sounding. We were impatient to start off, for sometimes we had to stand for hours, so we would sit down. And when the word was given; we used to spring forward as gaily and eagerly as if there were no cannon balls, bayonets, or bullets. I believe that so long as we felt our rider firm in the saddle, and his hand steady on the bridle, not one of us gave way to fear.

'I, with my noble master, went through many actions without a wound, though I saw horses shot down with bullets, pierced through with lances, and gashed with fearful sabre-cuts – and pay cuts; though we left them, dead men in the field, or dying in agony of their wounds, some lingered on long enough to draw their pay. My master's cheery voice encouraged his men: "Go on! Kill! Kill! Kill!" I saw many brave men cut down, many fall mortally wounded from their saddles. I heard the cries and groans of the dying. "Ohh, help, arghh, ouch, yaroo!" I had cantered over ground slippery with blood, mud and custard, and frequently had to turn aside to avoid trampling on wounded man or horse or custard.

'But one dreadful day, we heard the firing of the Russian guns. "Bangski! Bangski! Bangski! Bangski!" One of the officers rode up and gave the word for the men to mount, and in a second every man was in a saddle. Some were so quick, they had squashed knackers.

'My master said, "We shall have a day of it, Bayard, my beauty." I cannot tell you all that happened that day, but I will tell of the last charge we made in front of the enemy's cannon. "Bangski! Bangski! Bangski! Bangski!" went the Russian guns. Many a brave man went down; some went up; some went sideways. Many a horse without a rider ran wildly through the ranks, and many a rider without a horse ran wildly through the ranks. Our pace and gallop became faster and faster, and as we neared the cannon, we were doing 150 miles per hour.

'My dear master was cheering on his comrades with his right arm raised on high when a cannon ball blew his head off. I tried to check my speed. The sword dropped from his hand; he did a backward somersault and fell to earth. I was driven from the spot where he fell. It was a tiny spot, three inches in diameter.

'I wanted to keep my place by his side, but under the rush of horses' feet, it was in vain. When they had finished, he was flat, flat as a piece of cardboard, and they rolled him up, took him off the battlefield, and posted him back to his widow.

'Other noble creatures were trying on three legs, and some on two, to drag themselves along; others were struggling to rise on their fore feet, as their hind legs had been shattered by shot, shit and shell. There were their groans, "Ohh, help, arghh, ouch, yaroo!" After the battle the wounded were brought in, and the dead were buried. Sometimes the wounded were buried by mistake.

'I never saw my master again because they buried him. I went into many other engagements – I did a week at the Palladium.'

I said, 'I have heard people talk about the war as if it was a very fine thing. They only say it before they go through hell.'

'Do you know what they fought about?' enquired a civilian.

'Yes,' I said, 'they fought about two years.'

I wondered if it was right to go all that way over the sea, on purpose, to kill Russians, and in return get killed yourselves.

Briefly they rode into the mouth of hell. But what was that terrible smell? It was the gallant six hundred.

35

JERRY BARKER

My new master wore a wig
It looked like a crow's nest made from bits of twig
One day a crow tried to lay eggs in the nest
To hatch the eggs, she tried her best
Alas, the nest was found by a pussy-cat
And that was that
My stable boy was always jolly
He wanted to do what he could, so he did it to Dolly.

Jerry Barker had tried to shoo the crow away with a cat-apult, but he rendered the crow unconscious just as an RSPCA crow warden came by who reported it to the police. He was charged with cruelty to a crow, fined five shillings, and sent for life to Van Demon's Land.

I never knew a better man than my new master; he was kind and good, and as strong for the right as John Manly; and so good-tempered and merry that few people could pick a quarrel with him. He was very fond of making up little songs and singing them to himself:

> Come, father and mother,
> And sister and brother,

Take all your clothes off
And do one another

Harry was as clever at stablework as a much older boy,
and always wanted to do what he could. He did it to
Dolly. Dolly and Polly used to come in the morning to
help with the cab – to brush and beat the cushions, and
rub the glass, while Jeremiah Barker was giving us a
cleaning in the yard and Harry was rubbing the harness.
Jeremiah Barker would say:

> If you in the morning
> > Throw minutes away
> You can't pick them up
> > In the course of the day.
> You may hurry and scurry,
> > And flurry and worry,
> You've lost them for ever,
> > For ever and aye.

It was poetry, but bloody dreadful.

He could not bear any careless loitering, and waste of
time – very much like Mrs Doris Wretch of 22 Gabriel
Street, Honor Oak Park – and nothing was so near making him angry as to find people who were always late,
wanting a cab horse to be driven hard, to make up for
their lateness.

One day, two wild-looking young men called, 'Hey
cabbie, look sharp, we are rather late; put on the steam,
will you, and take us to Victoria in time for the one
o'clock train? You shall have a shilling extra.'

Larry's cab was standing next to ours; the bastard

flung open the door and said, 'I'm your man, gentlemen! Take my cab, my horse will get you there all right,' and he shut them in, with a wink towards Jeremiah Barker. Then, slashing his jaded horse, he set off as hard as he could. Jerry patted me on the neck – 'No, Jack, a shilling would not pay for that sort of thing, would it, old boy?'

Although Jeremiah Barker was determinedly set against hard driving to please late people, still they used to walk to their work, often being killed under horses and carriage.

I well remember one morning, as we were on the stand waiting for a fare: he did not know why a young man, carrying a portmanteau, tripped over a banana skin (that Jeremiah had specially placed there) and fell down with great force, with the portmanteau on top of him.

Jeremiah Barker was the first to run and lift him up, and led him into a shop. He came back to the stand, but in ten minutes one of the shop men called him, so he drew up.

'Can you take me to the South-Eastern Railway?' said the young man. 'I fear it is of great importance that I should not lose the twelve o'clock train.'

'You can't lose a train,' said Jeremiah, 'it's too big.'

'If you could get me there in time, I will gladly pay you extra.'

'I'll do my very best,' said Jeremiah Barker, heartily, 'if you think you are well enough, sir.'

'Now, then, Jack, my boy,' said Jeremiah Barker, 'spin along; we'll show them how we can get over the ground.'

On Jeremiah Barker's return to the rank, there was a

good deal of laughing, highland dancing and chaffing at him for driving hard to the train.

'Gammon!' said one. (He meant Mammon, the ignorant bastard.)

'If you ever do get rich,' said Governor Gray, looking over his shoulder across the top of his cab, 'you'll deserve it, Jerry. As for you, Larry, you'll die poor, you spend too much in whipcord.'

'Well,' said Larry, 'what is a fellow to do if his horse won't go without it?'

No good luck had Larry
He couldn't afford to marry
He longed for a busty bride
Alas, his fortune was at low tide
The nearest he could get to a busty girl
Was screwing a local barmaid called Pearl
Her father caught them screwing on the grass
So he gave Larry a kick in the arse.

36

THE SUNDAY CAB

He was regretting not working on day seven
Even tho' the rule had been made in heaven
Turning down Mrs Muir's cash
Was a decision oh, very, very rash
He and his family were starving, to refill the larder
He'd have to work a lot bloody harder.

One morning, as Jeremiah Barker had just put me into the shafts and was fastening the traces, a gentleman walked into the yard. 'Your servant, sir,' said Jeremiah Barker.

'What about my servant, Mr Barker?' said the gentleman. 'I should be glad to make some arrangements with you for taking Mrs Briggs regularly to church.'

'Thank you, sir,' said Jerry, 'but I have only taken out a six day licence, and therefore, I could not take a fare on Sunday.'

'Oh!' said the other, and did a backward somersault. 'I did not know yours was a six day cab; but of course it would be very easy to alter your licence. I would see that you did not lose by it; the fact is, Mrs Briggs very much prefers you to drive her. Of course,' said Mr Briggs, 'I should have thought you would not have minded such a short distance for the horse, and only once a day.'

'Yes, sir, that is true, and I am grateful for all favours, and anything I could do to oblige you, or the lady, I should be proud and happy to do.' He was now prostrate on the ground, placing Mr Briggs' boot on his head. 'But I cannot give up Sundays, sir.'

'Very well,' said Mr Briggs, 'fuck you, and your horse.'

'Well,' says Jeremiah Barker to me, 'we can't help it, Jack, old boy, we must have our Sundays.'

'Polly!' he shouted. 'Come here this minute.'

She was there that minute.

'What is it all about, dear?'

'Why, my dear, Mr Briggs wants me to drive on a Sunday.'

'I say, Jerry,' she said, speaking very slowly, 'I say, if Mrs Briggs would give you a sovereign every Sunday morning, I would not have you a seven day cabman again. We have known what it was to have no Sundays; and now, thank God, you earn enough to keep us, though it is sometimes close work to pay for all the oats and hay, the licence and the rent besides, and we only have oats for dinner.'

Three weeks had passed away, but Mr Briggs didn't. What a bloody fool Jeremiah's wife was, to encourage him not to drive on a Sunday. For the last week they had been having hay for dinner.

> Oh, terrible only having hay for dinner
> That's why they were all getting thinner
> By not driving on the seventh day

He was losing money, they say
Not only losing money, they state
But also rapidly losing weight
He on his own
Barely weighed five stone
To prevent him being blown off the box
In his boots, they had to put rocks.

But Polly would always cheer him up and say:

'Do your best,
And leave the rest,
'Twill all come right,
Some day or night.'

'What a lot of bollocks,' he thought, as he put more rocks in his boot.

It soon became known that Jerry had lost his best customer, and for what reason; most of the men said he was a fool, but two or three took his part. Where they took his part, or which part, is unknown.

Jeremiah Barker had promised on Sunday not
to drive
So he couldn't go anywhere, leave alone a
ride
He would lose the trade of Mrs Briggs
Whose custom helped them pay for the digs
Losing his customer would lose him money
Something he didn't think very funny.

37

THE GOLDEN RULE

Oh, hurrah, hurrah for Mrs Briggs
Whose money helped pay for their digs
She wants Jerry's cab for hire again
But never on Sundays for shame
She only wanted him on a Monday
Which is dangerously near Sunday
The Barkers were happy to say
'Thank God, we don't have to eat hay'
Three cheers – Hip, Hip, Hooray.

Two or three weeks after this, as we came into the yard, Polly came running across the road with a lantern in bright sunshine. It made her feel safe.

'It has all come right, Jerry; Mrs Briggs sent her servant this afternoon to ask you to take her out tomorrow. She says there is none of the cabs so nice and clean as yours, and nothing will suit her but Mr Barker's.'

'Oh, I'd better get all the crap out of it then. The last customer had sheep with him.'

Jerry broke out into a merry laugh: 'Ha hah hee hee oh ha ha ha oh ha ha ha. Run in and get the supper.'

After this, Mrs Briggs wanted Jerry's cab quite as often

as before; never, however, on a Sunday; but there came a day when we had Sunday work.

'Well, my dear,' said Polly, 'poor Dinah Brown has just had a letter brought to say that her mother is dangerously ill, she's got piles and nothing can get through. It's only half Sunday without you, but you know very well what I should like if my mother was dying of piles.'

'Why, Polly, you are as good as the minister, but a terrible accountant. Go and tell Dinah I will be ready as the clock strikes ten; but stop!' Polly stopped. 'Just step round to the butcher and ask for a meat pie to be put away.'

She went and came back and said, 'That will be a pound for the meat pie.'

'Well tell the swine he shouldn't be doing business on a Sunday. Fog will strike him dead for selling a God-fearing woman a meat pie on the Sabbath. Now put me up a bit of bread and cheese, and I'll be back in the afternoon.'

'And I'll have the meat pie ready for an early tea, instead of for dinner.'

'Oh no! Not again!' said Jeremiah.

Dinah's family lived in a small farmhouse, up a tree, close by a meadow: there were two cows feeding in it.

'There is nothing my horse would like better than an hour or two in your beautiful meadow,' said Jeremiah.

'Do, and welcome,' said the young man. 'We shall be having some dinner in an hour, and I hope you'll come in; we will lower a rope and pull you up.'

Jeremiah thanked him, but said he would like nothing better than to walk around the meadow with meat pies in his pocket. He picked flowers in the meadow. When he got back he handed Dolly the flowers; she jumped for joy. She cleared the dining table with six inches to spare.

'Your meat pie is ready,' she said.

'Oh Christ,' said Jeremiah, and hurled it out the window.

38

DOLLY AND A REAL GENTLEMAN

Oh terrible carter, whipping his steed
His were sinful deeds
To his horses, which numbered two
A man tried to stop him and was struck down
He was wearing a suit of brown
He told the police, despite being frail
So the carter will wind up in jail
Before that, one recalls
His horse kicked him in the balls.

The winter came in early April, with a great deal of cold and frost. Jeremiah Barker's things were all shrivelled up. There was snow or sleet or rain, almost every day for weeks, changing only for keen driving winds, or sharp frosts. The horses all felt it very much. I felt mine and it felt frosty.

When we horses had worked half the day we went to our dry stables, and could rest. I would get in my bed and pull up the blanket. The drivers would sit on their boxes until two in the morning if they had a party to wait for. It was usually the Conservative Party, and they were so pissed none of them knew where they lived.

When the weather was very bad, many of the men

would go and sit in the toilets in the tavern close by, and get someone to watch for them; why they wanted someone to watch for them in the toilet seems a perversion. Jeremiah never went to the Rising Sun, but he went to the toilet; he resented drink. It was his opinion that spirits and beer made a man colder, and pissed. He believed in dry clothes, good food, cheerfulness and a comfortable wife at home, none of which were available at the Rising Sun. Polly always supplied him with something to eat – meat pies. Sometimes, he would see little Dolly peeping from a crack in the pavement to make sure if father were on the stand. If she saw him, she would run off at speed and come back with something in a tin or basket – a meat pie. It was wonderful how such a little thing could get across the street, often thronged with horses and carriages, and police dynamiting a way through; but she was a brave little maid, and felt it quite an honour to bring 'father's first course', as he used to call it. She was a general favourite on the stand, and there was not a man who would not have seen her safely across the street – they threw her.

One cold windy day, Dolly had brought Jeremiah something hot – it was a meat pie – and was standing by him to make sure he ate it all. He had scarcely begun, when a gentleman walked towards us very fast, so fast he went past us and had to back up. He held up his umbrella. Jeremiah touched his hat in return, gave the meat pie to Dolly, and was taking off my cloth, when the gentleman cried out, 'No, no, finish your meal, my friend.'

'It's all right, my daughter is finishing it for me.'

He asked to be taken to Clapham Common. I think

he was very fond of animals because when we took him to his own door, a zebra and two hyenas came bounding out to meet him. This gentleman wasn't young, he was about 104. There was a forward stoop in his shoulders, as if he was always going into something, like walls, trees, lamp posts and zebras.

The gentleman stopped at a veterinary surgeon to take his huge tomcat in for an operation. The window was full of clocks and watches. When the tom's operation was finished, he said, 'Why have you got your window full of watches and clocks?'

The veterinary surgeon said, 'What would you put in the window?'

There was a cart, with two very fine horses, standing on the other side of the street. I cannot tell how long they had been standing. (They had in fact been standing there for seven months.) They started to move out, the carter came running out, and with whip punished them brutally, beating them about the head. Our gentleman saw it, and stepping quickly across the street, was immediately knocked down. From the prone position he said:

'If you don't stop that directly, I'll have you summoned for leaving your horses, for brutal conduct, knocking me to the ground and displacing my false teeth.'

The man must have been doing the white-eared elephant, as his trouser pockets were pulled inside out, his flies were open and his willy was hanging out.* The man poured forth some abusive language, but he left off

*A coarse soldier entertainment.

knocking the horses about. The gentleman took the number of the cart.

'What do you want with that?' growled the carter.

The gentleman replied, 'I'm going to report you for doing the white-eared elephant without a licence.'

The carter was fined a million pounds, hung and deported to Bexhill for life.

39

SEEDY SAM

Poor, poor Seedy Sam
Said, 'Oh, what an unlucky bastard I am
I've the arse out of my trousers
I can't afford to buy any fresh horses
Driving out in the wind and rain and ice
Is not very nice
How long I can carry on I don't know
At any moment I can go
I nearly went yesterday
So the end can't be far away.'

I should say, that for a cab horse, I was very well-off indeed; my driver was my owner, and it was in his interest to treat me well, and not overwork me, otherwise (1) I would have kicked him in the balls, (2) I would have trampled on his head.

One day, a shabby, miserable-looking driver who went by the name of Seedy Sam (he had the arse out of his trousers, actually he had his arse out of *somebody else's* trousers), brought in his horse which was so ill, he was carrying it over his shoulder. The Governor said:

'You and your horse look more fit for the knackers.'

The man flung his tattered rug over the horse, put some sticks around it to hold it up, turned full round upon the Governor and said, in a voice that came from the arse out of his trousers:

'If the knackers have any business with the matter, it ought to be with the masters (cough, cough) who charge us so much, or with the fares that are fixed so low. You know how quick some of the gentry are to suspect us of cheating (cough, cough, cough) and over-charging; why, they stand with their purses padlocked in their hands, counting it over to a penny, and looking at us as if we were pickpockets (cough, gob, cough, cough, cough, gob).'

The men who stood round much approved his speech and his display of coughing and gobbing.

My master had taken no part in this conversation. He was willing to take the part of Joseph of Nazareth, but nobody had asked him.

A few mornings after this talk, a new man came on the stand with Sam's cab.

'Halloo!' said one, 'what's up with Seedy Sam?'

'He's ill in bed,' said the man. 'His wife sent a boy this morning to say his father was in a high fever and could not get out.'

The next morning the same man came again.

'How is Sam?' enquired the Governor.

'He's gone,' said the man.

'What? He's gone without telling us? That's not fair.'

'He died at four o'clock this morning, then five, then six; finally, at eight, he snuffed it. All yesterday he was raving (cough, cough), raving (cough, cough), raving (cough, cough).'

The Governor said, 'I tell you what, mates, this is a warning for us. If we want to go on working, we must avoid death.'

40

POOR GINGER

One day, I saw a horse in a state
I thought I better wait
It turned out to be Ginger, my friend
He was coming to a terrible end
He threw his legs around me and cried
'Oh, I wish I'd died'
His tears flooded the floor
I was forced to say, 'Stop crying, no more
We're drowning by the score.'

One day, a shabby old cab drove up beside ours. The horse was an old worn-out chestnut, with an ill-kept coat; you could see the lining, and bones that showed plainly through it. The knees knuckled over, and the forelegs were very unsteady. He was the worst case of horseitis I had ever seen. I had been eating some hay, and the wind rolled a little lock of it that way, and the poor creature put out his long thin neck and picked it up. There was a hopeless look in the dull eye that I could not help noticing, and then, as I was thinking, he looked full at me and said, 'Black Beauty, is that you?'

It was Ginger! But how changed! The beautifully arched and glossy neck was now straight and lank, and fallen in; the clean straight legs and delicate fetlocks were swelled; the joints were grown out of shape with hard work; the face, that was once so full of spirit and life, was now full of suffering, and I could tell by the heaving of his sides, and his frequent cough, how bad his breath was. It was the worst case of horse halitosis I had ever known. It was a sad tale that he had to tell.

After twelve months at Earlshall, he was considered to be fit for work again. In this way he changed hands several times, but always getting lower down.

I said, 'You used to stand up for yourself if you were ill-used, and kick them in the balls.'

'Ah!' he said, 'I did once; no, wait, I did it fifteen times. I wish the end would come, I wish I was dead. I wish I may drop down dead at my work.'

I waited for him to drop dead, but he didn't. He said, 'I don't feel like dropping dead today.'

A short time after this, a cart with a dead horse in it passed. The head hung out of the cart-tail, the lifeless tongue was slowly dripping with blood; and the sunken eyes! He would soon be a dinner in some French restaurant. It was a chestnut horse with a long thin neck. Wait! I saw a white streak down the forehead. It *was* Ginger; I hoped it was, for then his troubles would be over. Soon, he would be a tin of cat food.

41

THE BUTCHER

The butcher was a prompt man
Delivering meat by horse or van
His delivery boy rode them very fast
The butcher said, 'If you go on like this he won't last'
The boy said, 'I have to deliver on time
I have to, so the customer can dine
If only they'd order in advance
We wouldn't lead this merry dance'
So he bought the boy a bike
'I hope,' said the butcher, 'this is something he'll like.'

We horses do not mind hard work if we are treated with a dinner at the Savoy, or taken to a music hall. I am sure that many are driven by quite poor men who have had a happier life.

It often went to my heart to see how the little ponies were used, straining along with heavy loads, wearing a truss over their hernias. We saw one doing his best to pull a heavy cart back to Africa with ten elephants.

Pulling ten elephants back to Africa
For a little ruptured horse is much too far

Try, try, try as they may
They'll be lucky to get as far as Herne Bay
The ruptured horse to Africa will never get
The best he can hope is to be put down by
    a vet.

I used to notice the speed at which the butcher's boy was made to go – 90 miles per hour. One day, we had to wait some time in St John's Wood; we were actually waiting for St John. There was a butcher's shop next door and, as we were standing, a butcher's cart came dashing up at 100 miles per hour. The horse was hot, and much exhausted; he hung his head down, his legs hung down, his body hung down. The lad jumped out of the cart and the master came out of the shop and was much displeased when the lad landed on him.

'How many times shall I tell you not to drive at 100 miles per hour?'

'So far twenty, sir,' said the lad.

'You ruined the last horse and broke his wind, it smelled terrible, and you are going to ruin this in the same way. If you were not my own son, I would dismiss you on the spot.' (His was another spot a foot in diameter.) 'It is a disgrace to have a horse brought to the shop in a condition like that; you are liable to be taken up by the police for such driving, and if you are, you need not look to me for bail, for I have spoken to you till I am tired.'

During this speech, the boy had stood by, still standing on the spot, sullen and dogged. It wasn't his fault.

'You always say, "Now be quick; now look sharp!" and when I go to the houses, one wants a leg of mutton for an early dinner, and I must be back with it in a quarter of an hour.'

Who ever thinks of a butcher? Some people do nothing but think of a butcher. In fact, there's a Think of Butchers Society.

There was a young costerboy who came up our street with sacks of potatoes and a gorilla. Apparently, some people love gorilla and chips.

There was an old man, too, who used to come up our street with a little coal cart; he wore a coal-heaver's hat and was black from the coal. Actually, he was Ugandan and they called him Ogu Amin; his father got rid of all the wogs in his country.

42

THE ELECTION

Our cab was out on Election Day
Politicians were trying to find their way
Jerry wouldn't let his cab be used
For drunken voters to abuse
He told them to go away
And they've never been seen from that day.

As we came into the yard one afternoon, Polly came out:

'Jerry! I've had Mr B. here asking about your vote. He wants to hire your cab for the election.'

'Well, Polly, I'm sorry but I don't want to put up with half-drunken voters. It would be an insult to the horse, and I should hate to drive an insulted horse.'

'I suppose you'll vote for the gentleman?'

'I shall not vote for him, Polly; you know what his trade is?'

'Yes. He exports veal calves to the continent.'

Every man must do what he thinks best for his country. Some did Barclay's Bank and got away with it.

On the morning before the election, Jeremiah was putting me into the shafts when Dolly came into the yard, sobbing and crying.

'Why, Dolly, what is the matter?'

'Those naughty boys have thrown rice pudding, peaches and cream and it is all over me, and they called me a little ragamuffin,' she said, eating as much of it as she could before it slid off.

'They called her a little blue ragamuffin father,' said Harry, also covered in rice pudding, peaches and cream, and looking very angry. 'But I have given it to them, they won't insult my sister again. I killed them.'

Jeremiah Barker kissed the child and said, 'Run in to mother, my pet, and tell her I think you had better stay at home today and help her eat the rest of the rice pudding, peaches and cream.'

Then, turning gravely to Harry:

'My boy, I hope you will always kill anybody who offends your sister.'

'Why, father, I thought blue was for Liberty.'

'My boy, Liberty does not come from colours; they only show party, and all the liberty you can get out of them is liberty to get drunk and throw rice pudding, peaches and cream at each other.'

'Oh, father, you are laughing.'

'No, Harry, I am serious; I'm only laughing to camouflage me being serious.'

At that moment, he was hit full in the face with rice pudding, peaches and cream.

43

A FRIEND IN NEED

One day in the City
Jerry saw a woman and took pity
She was in the city all alone
She had a child weighing nineteen stone
She said she had to be at St Thomas by midday
So Jerry took her right away
From her, he refused to take her fare
The bloody fool, she was a millionaire.

At last came election day; there was no lack of work for
my master and me. First came a stout puffy gentleman
with a carpet bag; he wanted to go to the Bishopsgate
Station, so we let him; then we were called by a party who
wished to go to the Regent's Park, so we let them. We
waited in a side street where a timid, anxious old lady was
waiting to be taken to the bank, which she held up. We
had to wait and take her back (she robbed it again), and
just as we had set her down, a red-faced gentleman with a
handful of papers came running up, out of breath. Before
Jeremiah could get down, he had opened the door, pop-
ped himself in, and called out, 'Bow Street Police Station,
quick!' So off we went with him, where he was arrested.

Then we saw a poor young woman carrying a heavy child – it weighed nineteen stone – coming along the street. She was looking this way, and that way, like she was watching a tennis match, and seemed quite bewildered. Presently, she made her way up to Jeremiah and asked if he could tell her the way to St Thomas's Hospital, and how far it was to get there. She had got an order for the hospital, for her little nineteen stone boy. The child was crying with a feeble pining cry.

'Poor little fellow!' she said, 'he suffers a deal of pain; he is four years old and can't walk any more than a baby; but the doctor said if I could get him into the hospital, he might get well.'

'Please, get in our cab and I'll drive you safe to the hospital: don't you see the rain is coming on?'

'No sir, no, I can't do that, thank you. I have only just money enough to get back with: please tell me the way.'

'Look you here, missis,' said Jeremiah, 'I've got a wife and dear children at home, and I know a father's feelings; in fact I felt my wife this morning; now get you into that cab and I'll run you there for nothing.'

'Heaven bless you!' said the woman, bursting into tears.

'There, there, cheer up, my dear, I'll soon take you there; let me put you inside.'

As Jerry went to open the door, two men, with colours in their hats and button-holes, ran up, calling out, 'Cab!'

'Engaged,' said Jeremiah, but one of the men, pushing past the woman, sprang into the cab, followed by the other. Jeremiah looked as stern as a policeman: 'This cab is already engaged, gentlemen, by that lady.'

'Lady!' said one of them. 'Oh, she can wait: our business is very important; we import rice pudding, peaches and cream.'

'All right, gentlemen, pray stay.'

He soon got rid of them with his pistol; he blew out their brains.

Jeremiah walked up to the young woman, who had just finished counting a thousand gold sovereigns. After this little stoppage we were soon on our way to the hospital and when there, Jeremiah helped the young woman out.

'Thank you a thousand times. I've never travelled with dead men before,' she said. 'I could never have got here alone.'

'You're kindly welcome, and I hope the dear nineteen stone child will soon be better; but for him, we would have got here faster.'

The rain was now coming down fast, 100 miles per hour, and just as we were leaving the hospital the door opened again, and the porter called out, 'Cab!' We stopped, and a lady came down the steps.

She put her veil back and said, 'Barker! Jeremiah Barker! Is it you? I am very glad to find you here; you are just the friend I want, for it is very difficult to get a cab in this part of London today.'

'I shall be proud to serve you, ma'am; I am right glad I happened to be here,' he grovelled, 'where may I take you ma'am?'

He had no idea who she was.

'To the Paddington Station, and then if we are in good time, as I think we shall be, you shall tell me all about Polly and the children.'

We got to the station in good time and, being under shelter, the lady stood a good while talking. Jeremiah told her about the rice pudding and peaches and cream attack. I found she had been Polly's mistress.

'How do you find the cab work suits you in winter? I know Polly was rather anxious about you last year.'

'Yes, ma'am, she was; I had a bad cough that followed me up quite into the warm weather, and when I am kept out late, she does worry herself a good deal.'

'Well, Barker,' she said, 'it would be a great pity that you should seriously risk your health in this work, not only for your own, but also for Polly and the children's sake: there are many places where good drivers or good grooms are wanted; and if ever you think you ought to give up this cab work, let me know.' She put something into his hand saying, 'There is five shillings each for the two children; Polly will know how to spend it.'

He kissed her shoes, and seemed much pleased, and, turning out of the station, we at last reached home, and I, at least, was tired.

44

OLD CAPTAIN AND HIS SUCCESSOR

Oh, terrible crash with a brewer's dray
It happened on a clear sunny day
It had crashed into a cab horse
And injured it of course
Old Captain was the victim of the crash
He came out in a nervous rash
The brewer had to pay compensation to Captain's
    master
For the brewer, it was a financial disaster.

Captain and Jeremiah Barker had taken a party to the great railway station over London Bridge; the cab was full; it was the Labour Party; and, coming back, the Conservative Party mined the train.

Somewhere between the Bridge and the Monument, Jeremiah saw a brewer's dray coming along, drawn by two powerful horses. The drayman was lashing his horses with his heavy whip; they started off at a furious rate, at 100 miles per hour; the man had no control over them, and the street was full of traffic; they were now travelling at 102 miles per hour; one young girl was knocked down and run over, and the next moment they dashed up against our cab; both the wheels were torn off, the cab was thrown over and the Labour Party were thrown out. Captain was dragged down, the shafts splintered, and one of them ran into his backside. My master, too, was thrown, but was only bruised; nobody could tell how he escaped; he always said 'twas a miracle.

When poor Captain was got up, Jerry led him home gently, and a sad sight it was to see the blood soaking into his white coat; they were catching it in a bucket and pouring it back in the hole it came out, so they plugged the leak with a cork. The drayman was proved to be very drunk, and was fined ten pounds and asked for time to pay. While he was waiting to pay, they hung him, and the brewer had to pay damages to our master. But there was no one to pay damages to poor Captain.

The farrier did the best he could to ease his pain and make him comfortable; they put him up at the Savoy. The fly had to be mended, and for several days I did not go out, and Jeremiah earned nothing. The first time we went to the stand after the accident, the Governor came up to hear how Captain was.

'He'll never get over it,' said Jerry, 'at least not for my work, so the farrier said this morning. He says he may do for carting and that sort of work. If there's one devil that I should like to see in the bottomless pit more than another, it's the drink devil.'

'I say,' said the Governor, 'I'm not so abstemious as you are, more shame for me.'

'Well,' said Jeremiah, 'why don't you cut with it, Governor? You are too good a man to be the slave to the drink.'

'I'm a great fool, Jerry; but I tried once for two days,

and I thought I should have died: to stop me dying, I drank a bottle of whisky; how did you do it?'

'I had hard work at it for several weeks; you see, I never did get drunk, but I found that I was not my own master, and that when the craving came on, I'd take off all my clothes and run a mile. I had to say over and over to myself, "Give up the drink or lose your soul." Then off I'd run another nude mile. But, thanks be to God and my dear wife, my chains were broken, and now for ten years I have not tasted a drop. But just in case, I still run a mile in the nude. Now I wish I'd never given up!'

'I've a great mind to try it,' said the Governor, 'for 'tis a poor thing not to be one's own master.' So off he went on a run for a mile in the nude.

At first, Captain seemed to do well, but he was a very old horse, and it was only his wonderful constitution, and his convalescence at the Savoy, that kept him up at the cab-work so long; now he broke down and had to be towed away. The farrier said he might mend up enough to sell for a few pounds, but Jeremiah said, 'no!' and he thought the kindest thing he could do for the fine old fellow would be to put a bullet through his head; he would make jolly good cat food.

The day after this was decided, Harry took me to the forge for some new shoes; when I returned Captain was gone, but on the farrier's shelf was sixty tins of cat food. He would have been pleased he could make some pussy cat happy.

Jeremiah had now to look out for another horse, and first he looked out the window but couldn't see one. He stood on the cliffs of Dover looking through a telescope for one. He soon heard of one through an acquaintance who was under-groom in a nobleman's stables; he put his ear to the acquaintance and through him, sure enough, he could hear a valuable young horse. But he had smashed into another carriage, flung his lordship out, and the coachman had orders to look round – he already looked round through over eating – and sell him as well as he could.

'I can do with high spirits,' said Jeremiah Barker, 'as long as he doesn't kick me in the balls.'

'He tries to, but he misses,' said the man.

Our governor (the coachman, I mean) had him harnessed in as tight and strong as he could; his four legs were tied together. My belief is, that is what caused the accident.

The next day, Hotspur came home; he was a fine brown horse.

'Hello Hotspur,' I said.

The first night, he was very restless; instead of lying down, he kept jerking his halter; surely he would go blind. However, the next day, after five or six hours in the cab, he came in quiet and sensible; the cabman had gained a good horse. He had cost Jeremiah nine pounds, and he had paid cash.

Hotspur thought it a great come down to be a cab-horse, and disguised himself as a donkey. In fact, he settled in well, and master liked him very much, and discarded his donkey disguise.

45

JERRY'S NEW YEAR

It was one New Year's day
Freezing weather was here to stay
We had a late pickup, eleven o'clock
We waited till it was two of the clock
Our customers came out and pee'd against a tree
By then, it was half past three
When they didn't want to go any more
It was half past bloody four
They said they hadn't the fare
So we didn't take them anywhere.

Christmas and the New Year are very merry times for some people to get pissed; but for cabmen and cabmen's horses it is no holiday. There are so many big parties, and big balls. Sometimes driver and horse have to wait for hours in the rain or frost, shivering with cold, and whilst the merry people within are dancing away to the music, cabmen outside are dying of hypothermia. I saw a horse standing till his legs got stiff with cold, ice and rheumatism; think of horses standing till their legs get stiff with cold, ice and rheumatism.

I had most of the evening work now, as I was well

accustomed to standing covered in ice, and Jeremiah was also more afraid of Hotspur taking cold – he didn't give a fuck about me. We had a great deal of late work in the Christmas week, and Jeremiah's cough was bad; he gobbed up huge things that looked like breaking eggs when they hit the pavement; but however late we were, Polly sat up for him with a meat pie, and came out with the lantern so he could see it.

On the evening of the New Year, we had to take two gentlemen to a house in the West End. We were told to come again at eleven. 'But,' said one of them, 'as it is a card party, you may have to wait a few minutes, but don't be late.'

As the clock struck eleven we were at the door, for Jerry was always punctual. The clock chimed the quarters – one, two, three, and then struck twelve, but the door did not open.

The wind had been very changeable, with squalls of rain during the day, but now it came on a sharp driving sleet, which seemed to come all the way round; it was very cold.

At a quarter past one, the door opened and the two gentlemen came out; they chipped at Jeremiah with ice picks till he was free, then told him where to drive, which was nearly two miles away. When the men got out, they never said they were sorry to have kept us waiting, but were angry at the charge. They had to pay for the two hours and a quarter waiting; but it was hard-earned money to Jeremiah.

At last we got home. He could hardly speak and I could hardly neigh; his cough was dreadful and he was gobbing great egg yolks. Polly opened the door with a meat pie and held the lantern for him.

'Get Jack something warm, then boil a pot of gruel, then put me in it.'

This was said in a hoarse whisper (I too had a horse whisper); he could hardly get his breath. Polly brought me a warm mash and spread it over my frozen bed. That made me comfortable, and then they locked the door.

It was late the next morning before any one came, and it was Harry. He cleaned us and fed us. He was very still, and neither whistled nor sang, but did some Russian dancing. At noon he came again, and gave us our food and water. This time Dolly came with him. She was crying, and I could gather that Jeremiah Barker was dangerously ill and broke. The doctor said it was a bad case; so did his bank manager.

So two days passed away, but he didn't, and there was great trouble indoors. We only saw Harry, and sometimes Dolly. I think she came for company, for Polly was always with Jeremiah, and he had to be kept very quiet. So they rendered him unconscious with a mallet.

On the third day, whilst Harry was in the stable, there was a tap on the door – why anybody wanted to put a tap on a door is strange – and Governor Grant came in.

'I want to know how your father is.'

'He's unconscious,' said Harry, 'they call it bronchitis.'

'That's bad, very bad!' said Grant, shaking his head; it fell off.

'Yes,' said Harry, 'and the doctor said that father had a better chance than most men, because he didn't drink.'

The Governor looked puzzled.

'If there's any rule that good men should get over these things, I am sure he will, my boy.'

Early next morning he was there again.

'Well?' said he.

'Father is better,' said Harry. 'Mother hopes he will get over it.'

'Thank God!' said the Governor, 'and now you must keep him warm, and that brings me to the horses; you see, Jack will be all the better for the rest of a week or two in a warm stable, and you can easily take him a turn up and down the street to stretch his legs; but this young one, if he does not get work, he will soon be all up end, and when he does go out, there'll be an accident.'

'I have kept him short of corn,' said Harry, 'but he's so full of spirit, it's coming out the back.'

'Just so,' said Grant. 'Now look here, will you tell your mother that I will come for him every day till something is arranged, and whatever he earns I'll bring your mother half of it, and that will help with the horses' feed. Your father is in a good club, I know, but that won't keep the horses, and they'll be eating their heads off all this time.' And without waiting for Harry's thanks, he was gone.

For a week or more he came for Hotspur, and drove him at 150 miles per hour until he settled down, and when Harry thanked him, or said anything about his kindness, he laughed it off, saying it was all good luck for him. Polly got half the takings, but he kept the bigger half; his horses were wanting a little rest, which they would not otherwise have had.

Jeremiah grew better, steadily; first his feet got better, then his legs, and finally his body and head. The doctor said that he must never go back to the cab work again if he wished to be an old man. The children had many consultations together about what father and mother would do, and how they could help to earn money. There was bank robbery, but that was too dangerous; the bank manager would recognise him and ask him to repay his overdraft.

One afternoon, Hotspur was brought in very wet and dirty. While Harry was sponging off the mud from Hotspur, Dolly came in, looking very full of something. It was cottage pie.

'Oh! Harry, there never was anything so beautiful; Mrs Fowler says we are all to go and live near her. There is a cottage now empty that will just suit us, with a garden, and a hen house, and apple trees, and everything, and her coachman is going away in the spring to be put down, and then she will want father in his place!'

'That's uncommon jolly,' said Harry, in old English, 'it will suit father. I'll be a groom, a gardener or a bank robber. We'll need money.'

It was quickly settled that the cab and horses should be sold as soon as possible.

This was heavy news for me, for I was not young – I was 79. Grant said he would take Hotspur, and there were men on the stand who would have bought me, but Jerry said No! The Governor promised to find a place for me where I should be comfortable, possibly the Ritz.

The day came for going away. Jerry had not been allowed to go out yet, and was chained to his bed just in case. Polly and the children came to bid me good-bye. 'I wish we could take you with us,' she said. Dolly was crying and kissed me, too, then they buggered off, and I was led away to my new place.

46

JAKES AND THE LADY

I was sold to a corn dealer and a carter, called Jakes
To serve them it took me all it takes
Going downhill he never put on the brakes
'With that load, your horse you'll kill '
Said a gentlewoman called Jill
'Keep quiet you silly girl'
She, with a karate hold, gave him a huge hurl
He landed over a mile away
It made my day
He ran away to Spain
And we never saw him again.

I was sold to a corn dealer for three and six a pound whom Jeremiah Barker knew and he thought I should have good food and fair work.

In the first he was quite right, and if my master had always been on the premises, I do not think I should have been over-loaded; but there was a foreman who was always hurrying and driving everyone, even Queen Victoria, and frequently, when I had quite a full load, he would order something else to be taken on. My carter said it was more than I ought to take, but the other always overruled him:

' 'Twas no use going twice when once would do, and he chose to get business forward.'

Jakes, like the other carters, always had the bearing rein up, which prevented me from drawing easily, and by the time I had been there three or four months, I found the work telling very much; I was shagged out.

One day, I was loaded more than usual, and too often, and part of the road was a steep uphill: I used all my strength and Vitamin B tablets, and some Horlicks, but I could not get on. This did not please my driver, and he laid his whip on badly.

'Get on, you lazy fellow,' he said, 'or I'll tweak your swannicles.' Oh, no! I'd do anything for him not to tweak my swannicles.

Again I took some Horlicks tablets, started the heavy load, and struggled on a few yards backwards; again the whip came down, and again, to soothe it, I struggled backwards. The pain of that great cart whip was sharp. I'd sue the makers of Horlicks. A third time he was flogging me cruelly, when a lady stepped up to him:

'Oh! pray do not whip your good horse any more. I am sure he is doing all he can; the road is very steep and I am sure he is doing his best.'

'If doing his best won't get this load up, he must do something more than his best; that's all I know, ma'am,' said Jakes, which was all he knew.

'But is it not a very heavy load?' she asked.

'Yes,' he said, louder, 'but that's not my fault, I must get on with it as well as I can.'

He was raising the whip again, when the lady threw him over her shoulder judo style; she was a sixth Dan.

'He cannot use all his power with his head held back, as it is with that bearing rein. If you take it off, I am sure he would do better – *do* try it,' she said persuasively, giving him a karate chop.

'Yes, ma'am,' said the terrified carter. The rein was taken off; what a comfort it was!

'Poor fellow! that is what you wanted,' said she.

Jakes took the rein – 'Come on, Blackie.' I put down my head, and threw my whole weight against the collar; I spared no strength; the load moved on, and I pulled it steadily up the hill – and then stopped to take a spoonful of Sanatogen.

The lady had walked along the footpath, and now came across the road, stopping only to throw the carter on his back.

'You see, he was quite willing when you gave him the chance; I am sure he is a fine-tempered creature, and I dare say he has known better days. You won't put that rein on again, will you?'

'Well, ma'am, I can't deny that having his head and Horlicks has helped him up the hill.'

'Is it not better?' she said. 'I thank you for trying my plan with your good horse. Good-day,' and with another soft pat on my neck, she stepped lightly across the path, and I ran over her.

I may as well mention here what I suffered at this time from another cause. I had heard horses speak of it; mine was a badly lighted stable; there was only one very small window at the end, and the stalls were almost dark. It very much weakened my sight, and when I was suddenly brought out of the darkness into the glare of sunlight, it was very painful to my eyes (I had to have glasses), and I drove into a shop-front window. However, I escaped without any permanent injury to my sight, and was sold to a large cab owner.

47

HARD TIMES

Now my new master was called Skinner
He wouldn't give you the price of a dinner
My driver was very, very cruel
All I had to eat was watery gruel
I became so very thin
You could see in
Coming down Ludgate Hill
I fell and became very ill
I wanted to die
But I don't think I'll try.

I shall never forget my new master; he had black eyes and ears and a hooked nose, his mouth was full of teeth locked on a cheese sandwich. His name was Skinner, and I believe he was the same man that poor Seedy Sam died for.

Skinner had a low set of cabs, so low that if you looked out the window you could only see the pavement. He was hard on the horses; in this place we had no Sunday rest.

Sometimes on a Sunday morning, a party of fast men would hire the cab for a day in France; four of them inside and another with the driver, and I had to take them to Calais. I had to swim the channel and back again and sometimes I had such a high fever that I caught fire and had to be put out. I could hardly touch my food because there wasn't any. How I used to long for the nice bran mash with whisky in it that Jeremiah used to give us on Saturday nights in hot weather – that used to cool us down. But here, there was no rest, and my driver had a cruel whip with something so sharp at the end that it sometimes drew blood; gradually I was becoming anaemic. He would even whip me under the belly, and flip the lash out at my head. Indignities like these took the heart and my liver out of me, but still I did my best and never hung back.

My life was now so utterly wretched that I wished I might drop down dead at my work and go to the great stable in the sky. I tried hard, but somehow couldn't drop dead. One day, it very nearly came to pass.

I went on the stand at eight in the morning and had done a good share of work, when we had to take a fare to the railway. A long train was just expected in, so my driver pulled up at the back of some of the outside cabs, to take the chance of a return fare. It was a very heavy train, it weighed 5,000 tons, and all the cabs were soon engaged. There was a party of four; a noisy, blustering man with a lady, a little boy, and a young girl, and a great deal of luggage. The lady and the boy got into the cab, while the man ordered the luggage. The porter, who was pulling about some heavy boxes, suggested to the gentleman, as there was so much luggage, whether he would not take a second cab.

'Can your horse do it?' enquired the blustering man.

'Oh yes, he did some down the road.'

He helped to haul up a box so heavy that I could feel the springs go down. Box after box was dragged up and lodged on the top of the cab. At last all was ready and, with his usual jerk at the rein, he drove out of the station.

The load was very heavy and I had had neither food nor rest since the morning, save a boiled egg; but I did my best, as I always had done. I got along fairly well till we came to Ludgate Hill. My feet slipped from under me, and I fell heavily to the ground on my side; I lay perfectly still; I had no power to move. Someone said, 'He's dead, he'll never get up again.' Good, I could stay here! Then I could hear a policeman giving orders, 'Get up!' Some cold water was thrown over my head and some cordial was poured into my mouth. I cannot tell how long I lay there, but I found my life coming back. After some more cordial had been given me, I staggered to my feet, and was gently led to some stables, where I was put into a well-littered stall, and some warm gruel and Horlicks were brought to me.

In the morning, Skinner came with a farrier to look at me.

'This is a case of overwork, and if you could give him a run off for six months, he would be able to work again.'

'Then he must go to the dogs,' said Skinner.

Upon advice, Skinner gave orders that I should be well fed and cared for. Ten days of perfect rest with plenty of good oats, hay, bran mashes and Guinness (all with boiled linseed mixed in them), did more to get up my condition than anything else could have done; those linseed mashes were delicious with malt whisky, and I began to think that, after all, it might be better to live. When the twelfth day after the accident came, I was taken to the sale. I felt that any change from my present place must be an improvement. They put a label on my neck: 'Horse for sale. Good for knacker's yard.'

48

FARMER THOROUGHGOOD AND HIS GRANDSON WILLIE

At the sale I was in with old horses in wheel chairs
Many were in need of constant care
One man said of me, 'He has known better days
Soon he'll have to wear stays'
'Grandpa,' said the boy, 'can't we buy him?'
'All right,' said Grandpa looking grim
He paid five pounds for me straight away
And I stayed with them for many a day.

At this sale, of course, I found myself in company with old, broken-down, dying horses – some lame, some broken-winded, some in wheel chairs going on eighty. There were poor men trying to sell a dead horse for three pence to the PAL dog food company. Some of them looked as if they had seen hard times; the hardest times were from midnight to six o'clock in the morning.

Coming from the better part of the fair, I noticed a man who looked like a gentleman farmer, with a young boy by his side. When he came up to me, he stood still. I saw his eye rest on me; I had still a good mane and tail.

'There's a horse, Willie, that has known better days.'

'Do you think he was ever a carriage horse?' asked the boy.

'Oh yes,' said the farmer, coming closer, 'he might have been anything when he was young. Look at his nostrils and his ears, the shape of his neck and shoulder; there's a deal of breeding about that horse.'

So the boy looked at my nostrils and ears and the shape of my neck and shoulder. 'Could not you buy him and make him young again?'

'My dear boy, I can't make old horses young; this one is knackered.'

He was wrong. I had never been knackered; I still had a complete set.

'Well, grandpapa, I don't believe that this one is old – he has a complete set. But do look at his mouth, grandpapa, I am sure he would grow young in our meadows.'

The man who had brought me for sale now put in his word.

'The young gentleman's a real knowing one, sir; I heard as how the veterinary should say – that a six months in bed would set him right up.'

'What is the lowest you will take for him?' said the farmer.

'Five pounds, sir; that was the lowest price my master set.'

' 'Tis a speculation,' said the old gentleman, shaking his head, but at the same time slowly drawing out his purse and taking the lock off. 'Have you any more business here?' he enquired, counting the sovereigns into his hand.

'No, sir, I can take him for you to the inn, if you please.'

'Do so, and give him a whisky and soda.'

The boy could hardly control his delight, so he was put in a straight jacket. The old gentleman seemed to enjoy seeing him trying to get it off. I had a good feed and a whisky and soda at the inn.

Mr Thoroughgood, for that was the name of my benefactor, gave orders that I should have hay, oats, halibut liver oil and three-egg omelettes every night and morning, the fun of the meadow during the day, and the run of the stable at night, and, 'You, Willie,' said he, 'I give him in charge to you.'

The boy was proud of his charge and undertook it in all seriousness; in fact he was a downright misery. There was not a day when he did not pay me a visit; he became a bloody nuisance, sometimes picking me out from amongst the other horses, and giving me a bit of carrot (what bloody good was that?), or something good, or sometimes standing by me whilst I ate my oats. He always came with kind words and caresses and, of course, I grew very fond of him. He called me Old Crony, the bastard, as I used to come to him in the field and follow him about. Sometimes he brought his grandfather, who always looked closely at my legs; he was kinky.

'Willie,' he would say, 'he is improving so steadily that I think we shall see a change for the better in the spring.'

The perfect rest, the good food, the soft turf and gentle exercise, and the idiot grandchild in a straight jacket, soon began to tell on my condition and my spirits. I had a good constitution from my mother, and I was never strained when I was young.

During the winter, my legs improved so much that I

used them when I went out. The spring came round, and one day so did Mr Thoroughgood, to try me in the phaeton. I was well pleased, and he and Willie drove me a few miles. I did the work with perfect ease; I even sang 'Good-bye Dolly Grey.'

'He's growing young, Willie; we must give him a little gentle work now – he can clean out the chicken house – and by midsummer he will be as good as that milkmaid with big boobs.'

49

MY LAST HOME

> One day I was all dolled up
> The groom was called Tim Nup
> I was to be sold to two ladies
> Very respectable, not at all shady
> They took to me right away
> That would be £5 to pay
> I thought the fee below my worth
> Because I was of noble birth
> It would have been very nice
> If £50 was my minimum price.

One day, the groom cleaned and dressed me in a suit with such extraordinary care that I thought some new change must be at hand; he trimmed my fetlocks and legs, passed the tarbrush over my hoofs, parted my fore-lock, and flattened it down with Macassar oil. I think the harness had an extra polish. Willie seemed half-anxious, half-merry as he got into the chaise with his grandfather.

'If the ladies take to him,' said the old gentleman, 'they'll be suited.'

We came to a pretty, low house with a lawn and shrubbery at the front, and a drive up to the door. Willie rang the bell and asked if Miss Blomefield or Miss Ellen was at home. Yes, they were. So, whilst Willie stayed with me, Mr Thoroughgood went into the house. In about ten minutes he returned, followed by three ladies. The younger lady – that was Miss Ellen – took to me very much; she said she was sure she would like me.

'You have always been such a good adviser to us about our horses, and sexual proclivities,' said the stately lady, 'we will accept your offer of a trial.' At the trial they were found Not Guilty.

One morning, a smart-looking young man who was held together with acne came for me. When he saw my knees, he said:

'I didn't think, sir, you would have recommended my ladies a horse with knock-knees.'

'You are only taking him on trial, young man, and if he is not as safe as any horse you ever drove, send him back,' said my master.

I was led home, placed in a comfortable stable, fed and left to myself. The next day, when my groom was cleaning my face, he said:

'That is just like the star that Black Beauty had; he is much the same height too.' He began to look me over carefully, talking to himself:

'White star in the forehead, one white foot on the off side, this little knot just in that place' – then, looking at the middle of my back – 'Good heavens! it must be Black Beauty; there is that little patch of white hair that John used to call Beauty's threepenny bit. It *must* be Black Beauty!' (Good heavens, it was Black Beauty!) 'Why, Beauty! Beauty! Do you know me? Little Joe Green, that almost killed you?'

I could not say that I remembered him, for now he was a fine-grown young fellow, with black whiskers and a man's voice, and cross eyes – no wonder he nearly killed me. He was Joe Green. I never saw a man so pleased. He was so pleased that he climbed a tree and jumped in the river; they had to drag the water.

'Give you a fair trial? I should think so indeed! I wonder who the rascal was that broke your knees, my old Beauty? You must have been badly served out there somewhere.'

Yes, out there somewhere, I was.

'Well, well, it won't be my fault if you haven't good times of it now. I wish John Manly was here to see you.'

He wished and wished, but John Manly didn't appear; mainly because he was dead.

In the afternoon, I was put into a low Park chair and pushed to the door. Miss Ellen was going to try me. I soon found that she was a good driver, and she seemed pleased with my paces. I heard Joe telling her about me.

'I shall certainly write to Mrs Gordon, and tell her that her favourite horse has come to us with knock-knees. How pleased she will be!'

The swine, how dare he give away my knock-knees. So the next day, I kicked him in the balls. It was like old times.

I have now lived in this happy place a whole year; I have my own bedroom with a bathroom ensuite. Joe is the best and kindest of grooms, but with the curse of cross eyes keeps missing me. My work is easy and pleasant (I help wash up in the kitchen), and I feel my strength all coming back. Mr Thoroughgood said to Joe the other day:

'He will last till he is twenty years old – perhaps more.'

My ladies have promised that I shall never be sold, and so I have nothing to fear; and here my story ends. My troubles are over, all over me, hah, and I am at home; and often, before I am quite awake, I fancy I am still in the orchard at Birtwick, standing with my old friends under the apple trees and Dick the plough throwing stones at us.